T0095627

THE
INTERCESSION
OF
GOD

THE
INTERCESSION
OF
GOD

• A Novel •

BRUCE J. BONAFIDE

ARCHWAY
PUBLISHING

Archway Publishing books may be ordered through booksellers or by contacting:

Archway Publishing
1663 Liberty Drive
Bloomington, IN 47403
www.archwaypublishing.com
1 (888) 242-5904

ISBN: 978-1-4808-7923-2 (sc)
ISBN: 978-1-4808-7922-5 (e)

Library of Congress Control Number: 2019908071

Print information available on the last page.

Archway Publishing rev. date: 8/28/2019

Dedication

This book is dedicated to those whose faith in God is not challenged by the negative events that occur in each of their daily lives. This book is also dedicated to those who continue their faith in God though horrific events in their lives could cause them to become disbelievers. There are those whose faith in God is so strong that even events outside the realm of their control, where they bear no fault in the devastation that has been thrust upon them or their loved ones, still believe in God. There are some who maintain a belief in God, though their lives offer little hope for them and their children. They suffer poverty, disease, hunger, life threatening disabilities but still believe. The creation of man brought about the battle between good and evil for the immortal soul of man. To those who believe that good will win out over evil this book is dedicated to you.

Introduction

It is sometimes difficult for some to understand that the finite mind of man can neither comprehend nor understand the infinite mind of God as to what was planned since the first day of creation. It is also difficult for others to understand that the *Free Will* of man was given to them by the Creator as the basis for man's salvation to allow man to freely chose to love, honor, and obey the Creator. Man was given, through *Free Will*, the opportunity to be a part of God's plan for the reunion of their immortal soul with the Creator. This opportunity is what life is all about as we freely choose the kind of life we want to live to be worthy of that reunion. The challenges of life in all forms, many that are not of our own making, are tests as to how we respond to those challenges. Those responses represent how we act out the use of our *Free Will*. The choice, though sometimes not easy, is a reflection to some degree between the right choice and the wrong choice. The right choice is one that is looked upon by God as one that finds favor with God, and the wrong choice is one that does not find favor with God.

God knows that man must have *Free Will* so that the soul, which is made in the likeness of God, will be worthy to reunite with the Creator at life's end. Without *Free Will*, man's soul is relegated to a state of existence that is not consistent with their creation in the likeness of God. But rather, some entity solely obedient to the Creator's dictates. Without *Free Will*, man's willingness to independently love, honor, and obey are meaningless. If man's love, honor, or obedience cannot be given freely, the relationship wanted by God between the Creator and the created will have been thwarted.

Man was not the first entity to be created by God. Before man's creation, that same driving force within God's divine nature created the heavenly entity we know as angels. God bestowed on the angels, together with their immortal souls, the gift of *Free Will*. The angels were created in a blessed state in which they were allowed to know God and all the wonders of God's creation. The *Free Will* given to the angels became their downfall as some sought to learn how they could themselves become God-like. In so doing, they broke the trust between God and angels. In the ensuing battle between those angels who had remained true to God and those who challenged God, God intervened and cast out of heaven these fallen angels. Their wrong choice became the basis of sin and the beginning of evil. Instead of seeking God's forgiveness in the abuse of their *Free Will*, these fallen angels believed they could establish their own kingdom and continue to challenge God. It was not in God's plan or time frame to rid creation of these fallen angels and God allowed them to exist. Thus came into existence the challenge of the goodness of God versus the evil of these fallen angels. The creation of man brought about the battle for mankind to choose between good and evil. The sin of mankind against God caused man to be cast into a state of deprivation as mankind would now have to live their life on earth instead of in paradise.

Appreciation

A sincere appreciation is made to my wife and children for their support, understanding, and input for the creation of this novel. They, more than all others, know of the frustrations I've shared with them of the growing strength of evil in the world and the increased corruption of mankind by their fellow man. I especially appreciate their support in helping to re-affirm that the final outcome in the great battle between good and evil is in the hands of mankind and that *Free Will* provides man the ability to choose between God and salvation, or Satan and damnation.

The encouragement of other members of my family, as well as friends, to put my thoughts into writing a novel of this nature is greatly appreciated and I hope that this novel in some way will teach others to understand that peace on earth is truly in the hands of mankind.

Prologue

This is the story of a man who had achieved every success in life as measured by society. He also maintained a deep-rooted belief in God that was nurtured by a loving Christian family since the day of his birth. Being tall, handsome, athletic, and intelligent were traits that easily made him popular and complimented his kind, generous, and outgoing manner. In every endeavor, he found success as a star athlete, honor student, and as a combat U.S. Marine who was decorated for his bravery on the battlefields in Afghanistan and Iraq. Later, after he completed law school, he was pursued by some of the top law firms in New York, Los Angeles, and Chicago. He was assured that a life of both wealth and fame, only dreamt about by few others, were his for the taking.

But, the experience of war, as with many, had changed his life forever as he saw man's inhumanity to man and the terrible destruction and suffering of not only men, but women and children as well. He saw the cruel and inhuman acts of atrocity that plagued the innocent caused by barbaric humans. He sought to better understand why this evil was allowed and why these evil acts seemed to grow in number and magnitude. After he returned from the battlefield, he saw more evil in our society in the decadent greed for money, influence, and power over those less fortunate. He would pray each day to God to help him understand why such evil was being allowed to exist and grow.

He sought help from his devout parents as well as his older brother, a parish priest, and even his younger sister, a Carmelite nun. He examined the well-ordered life that all his talent and opportunity would afford him and he prayed that he would find a worthy purpose in life. Yet, he realized that all the success he could one day enjoy would not erase the many nights where his dreams became so real that he would awake in terror at the sights of children being mutilated as he had seen on the battlefield. Further, he saw indifference by those in power in their failure to come to terms with the evil in our society. Even in the land of the free and the home of the brave, he saw secularism allowing evil to grow and prosper.

He tried in his prayers to ask God for answers as to why the all-powerful Creator and a God that was all good would allow such evil to persist. Each day and each night no answer would come forth and all too often those nightmares would return in the form of a soldier's prayer for the battle to end.

> Deep in my fox hole I knelt and prayed
> Deep in my fox hole is where I stayed
> The sky was dark high overhead
> As I knelt there counting a thousand dead
>
> Through mud and rain and torn terrain
> We fought and struggled for sake of gain
> And gain we did, and again we gained, till
> Our mouths were dry, and clothes bloodstained
>
> But rise again to fight some more
> To gain some ground on this earthly floor
> Inch by inch and yard by yard
> Our men fell dead and our bodies scarred
>
> We reached the crest with a thousand less
> Our hearts were torn, as our minds were scorned
> As we all knelt and prayed
> For it was time to mourn

When Gabriel Bonaci woke each day, he knew he was one of the lucky ones who had returned home. The scars in his mind were not as visible as the scar where the bullet had torn through his shoulder that had now healed. He knew that for his mind to heal he must heal his soul first and come to terms with God and demand an answer as to why evil in the world was allowed to persist. Little did Gabriel realize that his sister, Sister Mary Theresa, would have the answer and the world would soon know what God had planned. Finally, Gabriel came to believe that a monastic life might enable him to rid himself of the horrors of war and the evil that permeated his mind and soul. He sought a place where he could find peace and the answers to God's apparent willingness to allow evil to exist and allow millions upon millions of souls to be lost due to the evils of mankind.

He retreated to a little monastery in Wisconsin, where as a monk he would have the solitude and time to reflect on his purpose in life.

Chapter One

More than 500 million years ago the terrain of Wisconsin was forever altered by the descending glaciers from the north. Today, on a former glacial hill, now the highest point in the state overseeing the surrounding countryside stands a magnificent basilica. The Holy Hill National Shrine of Mary has been a place of worship for more than one hundred and forty years. Here, the Carmelite nuns and friars with their history dating back to its religious affiliation with the order of the Holy Mother and Saint Teresa of Jesus, is where our story begins. Gabriel Bonaci, now a Benedictine Monk, recalls as a child visiting this site when there was no massive basilica but a small chapel and several small grottos with hundreds of steps ascending the hill on which the faithful would kneel in prayer at each step to reach the summit. There at the summit, a fifteen foot tall white cross surveyed the surrounding countryside.

Today, the convent of Our Lady of Sorrows nestled in the Kettle Moraine area of Holy Hill, Wisconsin houses the Carmelite nuns. This Catholic religious order is dedicated to good works of charity and self-sacrifice to the hundreds of thousands of the faithful that visit the basilica each year. Some of the faithful are merely there to visit the grandeur of the basilica. Some come to pray and others come in the hope that in response to their devotional prayers, a miracle will enable some to walk again or be cured of a life-threatening ailment. Others seek miracles to restore their sight as has occurred countless times over the past one hundred and forty years.

There, in one of the many small chapels that now make up part of the huge complex of the basilica and surrounding buildings, Sister Mary

Theresa Bonaci kneels in prayer. The chapel is simple, especially compared to the shrine on Holy Hill where the huge cathedral now houses the small fifteen foot white cross that once was the center of this religious site. Though only twenty- five years of age, she was now entering her eighth year of service since entering the convent as a novitiate. She knows little of the evil in the world that her brother Gabriel has shared with her. To her, the evil that does abound, is in the lack of food, clothing, and shelter that she and her fellow nuns seek to alleviate for the less fortunate. To her, evil is the disease that ravages the young and old that are taken before their time with some having barely left their mother's womb. Sister Mary Theresa is not a cloistered nun with little or no contact with the outside world as once had been her order's role. Her religious order had adapted to modern times under the new proclamations of the church in their efforts to serve those in the nearby communities.

Sister Mary Theresa is one the few younger nuns who are visible and interactive in the community. While her garb is simple, modest, and functional, some of the older sisters of the order continue to wear the black habits that envelop them from head to toe to reveal little but their hands and face. She wears no tunic but a plain ankle length skirt, long sleeve blouse and a long bolero vest with comfortable shoes. For the past two years, she has been one of a small group who often ventures out into the community to assist some of the small parishes that need help in serving the hungry, homeless, or homebound.

College-educated with a major in communications, Theresa knew from an early age that she had the calling to a religious life as she enjoyed camaraderie with other young girls who were mentored and guided into a religious vocation. Beyond her strong religious beliefs, she enjoyed a normal childhood of a girl who was popular among both genders who appreciated her friendly, warm, and engaging personality. Her maturity seemed well beyond her chronological age and her intelligence and wit often left the young girls, and especially the young boys, somewhat taken aback by her confident and forthright manner.

She was serious in her studies and was recognized for her leadership skills. She was often chosen as class officer, student council member, and yearbook editor. She was not shy, nor was she aggressive but well liked by all she met. She was tall and slender on her five foot eight inch lanky frame and she was considered by most to be pretty. She was neither aware of that fact, nor did she make any effort to adorn herself with makeup, or have any interest in fads or fashions that occupied much of her peer's fascination. As she got older, she seemed oblivious to the attentions of her male counterparts. Though she was always friendly and comfortable in their presence, she never gave any of them any encouragement by graciously saying no to their later requests for dates or wanting to spend individual time with her.

Her devout family directed her toward other interests, but as she grew older she chose a religious life versus the traditional life of marriage or a career in other fields. Theresa was strong- willed but gracious when others would question her calling or attempted to dissuade or demean her commitment to the chosen direction of her life. From a very early age, Theresa was drawn to the holy family and especially to devoting her life to being the bride of Christ. At first this concerned her parents, so they attempted to ensure that she had a healthy interest in the world. While she was exposed to various other interests and careers, she was instilled with the knowledge of the beauty of marriage between a man and a woman. She took an active interest in sports and the outdoors as a means to draw her into other activities that would engage her in a healthy interaction with other children and later, teens of her age.

Behind closed doors or in her private moments in chapel, especially praying at the Stations of the Cross, Theresa had the ability to block out the world about her as she was transfixed in prayer. When in prayer, it was as though she was being carried to another dimension and transformed into a state of almost unconscious focus in her adoration and prayer. The radiance in her face and the glow of an aura surrounding her in prayer lifted her heart, mind, and soul as she prayed. When she prayed, no spoken words ever left her lips, nor was a sound uttered. But, what was seen in her eyes, were expressions of sadness, pain, and torment. In her prayers, she asked that the hunger that she had seen in the faces and bodies of some she served, especially in the children, be experienced by her. She asked God to allow her to feel their hunger and the malnourishment that their bodies endured. In her prayers, she asked that she feel the desperation of their spirit in their feelings of loneliness and abandonment by society. She asked that the pain and discomfort of those ill and ridden with disease, whose strength had been sapped rendering them incapacitated, be visited upon her.

Yet, in her prayers she also gave thanks for the joy she felt at the birth of a child. She enjoyed watching them grow, giving her an understanding of the blessings of motherhood, and knowing that another spirit and soul was joined in Christ. In her prayers, she asked for guidance and strength to bolster her spirits to ward off any doubt in her beliefs, and to know compassion for the suffering of others. She asked for the infusion of the Holy Spirit to strengthen her against evil so that she would not succumb to the frailties of other humans and their weakness to the sins against God. She prayed to God to ask Mary, the Mother of God, to guide her in her devotion to God and to be a worthy bride of Christ.

But mainly, Theresa prayed to Jesus that He fill her with the Holy Spirit to show her a capacity to love beyond any human comprehension so she could offer that love to Jesus in servitude, obedience and humility. What Theresa did not know, was that God had directed at the time of her birth, that she be granted a special guardian angel that was powerful with God. This angel had been there at the time of the birth of Christ and throughout His ministry, crucifixion, resurrection and ascension into heaven. The Lord looked with favor on Theresa as she grew in purity of spirit. He tasked this angel to watch over her, so Theresa would become a beacon for women to be drawn to Christ, to create an assemblage of souls who would chose Christ on the Day of Judgment.

Her guardian angel protected her and watched out for her and guided her. As with all humans, evil lurked in the dark corners of her life as temptations of all kinds were able to be rooted out and thwarted by Theresa as she continued in her love of Christ. Though her Free Will was never compromised, Theresa had the propensity to always do what was right in the eyes of God. Theresa walked in the path of the Lord and all in heaven rejoiced. But one day, it would all change and "The Intercession of God" would be the answer that Brother Gabriel had sought all his life.

In the little town of Benet Lake, Wisconsin, right on the shores of Lake Benet sits St. Benedict's Abby. This monastery has its history dating back to only 1945 as reflected in its modern architecture and impeccable grounds. It is now the home of Brother Gabriel Bonaci. Gabriel has seated himself, as he most often does, to the rear of the chapel in a corner where a huge marble pillar blocks him from the view of others attending services but with a clear view of the crucifix that hangs from ornate chains above the alter.

It was obvious that Gabriel was not intent in prayer, but if he was, these prayers to God were not of a pious nature. His hands were not together in prayer and his arms hung down at his side with clenched fists. He wore a sullen expression on his face and his clenched teeth caused the muscles in his neck to be so pronounced that his veins were visible. He was in conflict, more so now than he had ever been since entering the monastery less than four years earlier. Gabriel was not a monk of the traditional sort having entered the monastic life at a far older age with a far different background than the other monks.

When Gabriel received his discharge from the Marines, he surprised everyone when he announced that he was pledged to join a monastery of the Benedictine Order to begin his religious training. During the war, Gabriel had an epiphany as to the futile nature of war and those who waged war for motives that had little to do with the protection and survival of their people. He had seen children and women with bombs strapped to their bodies that were prepared to blow themselves up and those around them. They believed that God wanted them to destroy themselves and others to achieve greater glory with God. Gabriel hated what was inside their minds that had taken away their innocence and twisted their faith to make them do these unspeakable acts. Human life had become worthless to them and their willingness to die without reason shook the very fiber of his core as to the purpose of this bloodshed.

Gabriel had pondered what he would do with the rest of his life once he came home from the battlefield. The great mystery of life as well as the purpose of his creation needed to be addressed. What would it matter for him to come home and become wealthy, powerful, and become a husband and a father? For what purpose would it be to watch his sons and daughters go off to war and die as more wars followed other wars. Did generation upon generations of men, women and children need to endure such futile deaths? One human could never become powerful enough to stop wars, only God could undertake such a task. Was Gabriel merely to become another cog in the wheels of humanity to live well while others suffered and to ignore the destruction and murder of those who were innocent victims?

He finally came to the realization that he had to take his concerns to the only one to whom those concerns could be addressed. He needed to take his case to the only one who could do something about it and that was at the court of the Supreme Being and find out from God Himself what could be done. Now, for almost four years he had been sitting in this very pew reaching out to God for hours, days, and months now extending into years of praying to God to answer his concerns only to receive no response. Joining the monastery had obviously not given him the answer. Now he was becoming bitter and angry and losing his faith in God as he continued to learn of more deaths, wars, and destruction. Society and mankind had not advanced one inch in eliminating evil, but instead had created weaponry that could kill people at a more rapid rate as greed for power, money, control, and subjugation persisted.

Suddenly, Gabriel felt a tap on his shoulder and turned to look up to Brother Mark. "Brother Gabriel, Father Jacob wants you to come to his office when you've concluded your prayers."

Brother Gabriel responded in an indifferent yet shocking tone, "I'm done praying to a deaf God!"

"Brother Gabriel," replied Mark, "God is not deaf to all who pray."

"Yes, yes, I'm sorry, I'll see Father Jacob immediately," murmured Gabriel.

Gabriel rose and left the chapel immediately. He knew that his good and positive attitude since arriving at the monastery had declined and not just Brother Mark was aware of his now more often belligerent comments. No doubt his attitude, just displayed to Brother Mark, would be a topic of conversation with Father Jacob. Gabriel knocked quietly on the office door and upon hearing the strong self-assured voice beckoning him in, he opened the door and entered. A softly lit room, with the morning light casting a beam of rays directly on Father Jacob, made it appear as if heaven had opened its firmament on the thin and somewhat fragile figure seated behind a huge desk. Gabriel was the first to speak, "You wanted to see me Father?"

"Yes Gabriel, please be seated."

Gabriel noted immediately that Father Jacob had not used the more formal title of Brother in addressing him. He knew that the ensuing conversation would be of a compassionate father to son tone, rather than a stern disciplinary lecture.

"Gabriel," Father Jacob continued, "you have been at the monastery for almost four years and while you've been an exemplary monk in all of your duties and tasks, it has not gone unnoticed that you are not happy in the monastic life you've chosen."

"Father, I'm not sure how to reply to that observation made by others within the monastery."

"Tell me my son, what is it that is troubling you these past several months? The enthusiasm with which you had embraced our order in your first three years seems to have waned considerably and I'd like to know the reason for the change."

"I'm sorry Father," Gabriel offered, "that I've become a source of concern to you and our fellowship. I love all of you and the change isn't about the monastic life as I welcome it and embrace it."

"Gabriel, when you first came to us and I learned of your background, I was surprised with your choice of vocation with us. Not many come to us with the opportunities you've been blessed with, my son. When you first came, I asked why you had chosen the monastic life and you said it was for the love of God. I was overjoyed with the simplicity and honesty of your answer. But, I should have asked you then, what that meant to you, so I'll ask you now."

Gabriel paused to consider his reply and the contemplative expression on his face signaled to Father Jacob that Gabriel understood that his answer must be meaningful and sincere. Finally, as Gabriel shifted in his chair under the patient and watchful eye of Father Jacob, he was able to summon from deep within himself those feelings that he had harbored for a long time.

"Father, all my life I've questioned the existence of God, but my family, especially my brother, a Jesuit priest and my sister, a Carmelite nun helped reinforce my belief in God. They did so with sound, almost scientific evidence. They explained how the known universe and all the intricacies of physics and nature defy any other rational explanation as to how the universe got here and how from nothing, did something occur. Plus, they reinforced logic with a huge bit of faith and shame for thinking to the contrary. Then, I discovered the 'Pascal Wager Theory.' Have you heard of it, Father?"

Father Jacob smiled, as he had often heard of this 'Pascal Wager Theory,' nodding his head in understanding. "Yes Gabriel, I have heard of this theory and I am well acquainted with the French philosopher and physicist and his many writings. But, I'd like to hear your take on what you understand that wager to be?"

"Well Father, the theory is that if one believes in God and in so believing lives a good life faithful to God for their temporal time on earth of maybe no more than one hundred years or less, they would enjoy an eternity in heaven. Or, the alternative is not believing in God and living a life of evil and choosing sin for their temporal time on earth. They would then be condemned to hell for all eternity. So which is better? The wager is that an eternity in heaven is a better wager than an eternity in hell. With my family's deep religious convictions and my own desire to believe in God, as well as believing that this wager theory has common sense merit, I was content with my belief in God."

"Well Gabriel, that theory, as theories go, is a weak argument as a reason to believe in God, but I grant you that it does have a beneficial outcome for your soul. In reading your biography when you first entered the monastery, I understood that in college you wrote a thesis called 'The Martian Mary Theory,' and though I was inquisitive at the time, I forgot all about it until now. Would you care to share with me the basis of that thesis?"

"Father, even as a senior in college I kept asking myself why, since the salvation of man had already occurred thousands of years before, God persisted in allowing more and more human souls to be born. What was God waiting for since mankind had pretty much ruined the earth and evil seemed to be having a field day. Why not bring about Judgment Day now rather than allow mankind and evil to persist for another two thousand years. I used to joke that another big reason to not believe in God, was how could God create the beautiful grandeur and majesty of Earth and then make the big mistake of creating humans to mess it all up. So I theorized that maybe humans on Earth were not the only creatures in the universe that God had created. Maybe these creatures on some distant planet had committed a sin for which they also needed salvation, as had occurred to humans on Earth. Due to the fact that salvation for man and man's atonement for God's forgiveness was needed, the Savior needed to be a God/man. Christ being God that became man made this all very possible because as God, all things are possible. But, for this God/man to truly be of man, Christ as God needed to take on the embodiment of man for man to receive God's forgiveness of man's sins. To do so, Christ needed to be born as a man and God chose the Blessed Virgin Mary to enable Christ the God to become Christ the man. In Christ's suffering and crucifixion, Christ as the God/man was able to atone for man's sins against God to once again allow for man's salvation."

"Gabriel, you were taught well by the Jesuits as to one of the great theologian mysteries that accompany the beliefs of the church regarding salvation and our belief in the Trinity of God. But, none of what I've just heard would result in your expulsion from the university."

"No Father, the reason for the expulsion came about when I extended that theory to say that God's creatures on other planets in the universe who also had been infused with a divine soul, undertook the same path of sinning against God as we did here on earth. This therefore required the same method of forgiveness and salvation through that same God/creature concept."

"I'm sorry Gabriel, usually I'm able to follow most theoretical thought, but this idea of God/creatures leaves me at a loss."

"Father, I'm sorry for giving you the shortened version of my twenty-page paper, but though Christ as God could travel the universe to all of such inhabited planets, Christ could not without the help of the Blessed Virgin Mary, have received the embodiment of man to make Christ the God, become Christ the God/man. But, Mary from earth could not give Christ the embodiment of a creature from a distant planet. Thus became 'The Martian Mary Theory' in which we would have many queens of heaven which relates to the fact that Mary could only be the sole mother of Christ the God/man on Earth and but not the Christ that becomes Christ the God/creature."

Father Jacob had sat silently listening to Gabriel's thesis unfold and took several moments to contemplate Gabriel's blasphemous theory before he replied in a calm and even voice. "I can see why the university suspended you and I'm equally interested in hearing how you were able to reconcile the conclusion to your theory with one that would conform to Catholic and Christian teachings."

"Father, do you remember the original question that had been put forth in the beginning of that theory?"

Father Jacob pondered the question for what seemed like an inordinate amount of time before replying, "Is the answer, why was God waiting so long after salvation to bring about the Final Day of Judgment while evil persisted to grow and the suffering of mankind continued?"

"Yes Father, in so many words. So, in my thesis, I had assumed that on each of the planets where God created these other-world creatures, He had infused them with the Holy Spirit and that they too had sinned as man had on earth. But, by the mystery of God, salvation did not come to these other planets but salvation had come only here on earth. These creatures, as the humans before Christ's birth, are waiting for the Savior to come. The mystery of why God had chosen a certain prophet, such as Moses over others, and why Mary was chosen over other women to be the Mother of God, is the same rational as to why God chose the Earth over all other places in the universe for salvation to occur. So," Gabriel continued, "the task given to mankind was when Christ asked His disciples to spread the word of God and salvation, God's message was not to just spread the word to the far corners of the Earth, but to the far corners of the universe to all of God's creatures infused with the Holy Spirit. Therefore, Judgment Day in God's time frame will not come until all in the universe know that salvation has come. Therefore, the Blessed Virgin Mary is truly the singular Mother of Christ the God/man that has brought salvation to all of God's creatures in the universe infused with God's spiritual likeness. Therefore, Mary is the true Queen of Heaven."

"I take it," Father Jacob concluded, "that your university accepted your revision and you were allowed to graduate?"

"Yes Father that was the case, but what is your opinion of my new thesis conclusion?"

"I believe that you have helped reinforce my thinking as to why we needed to have this meeting and conversation," replied Father Jacob. "But, tell me Gabriel, what is really troubling you?"

"Father, all my life I've questioned the existence of God at many turns in my life, but it was only after I returned from the war that I concluded that there was no God. Deep within me I knew that there had to be a God so I shifted my thinking that if there is a God, it's a God that doesn't really care. He is not a God that is active in our lives or involved with what is going on in the world. Later, as I came to understand Christ's birth, crucifixion, resurrection, and ascension, I came to see Christ as the affirmation of God's willingness to become involved in his creation."

"Tell me Gabriel, what then changed your thinking?"

"During the war, I continued to see evil persist over good and evil grow and multiply. I saw other supposed religions expand to millions upon billions of people who did not espouse the Judeo/Christian beliefs in the Bible. While at the same time, Christianity seemed to be in a steep decline. I saw that Christ was not involved in the day to day relevancy of life. I saw the genocide, the wars, and millions of suffering innocent children that were starving and dying. They were not even given the chance of Free Will to live their lives or realize the opportunity for them to know Christ."

"So, why Gabriel did you come to us and our monastic order? What were you seeking and what did you hope to find among us?"

"I came here Father to better understand God, and for Christ to intercede for me to know and understand the mind of God as to why God allows all this evil in the world."

"Gabriel, Gabriel, you took a vow of obedience to be faithful to God. What did that vow mean to you? Do you not think that others before you did not have the same thoughts and same feelings as you've had? Is your vow of obedience and belief in God in the face of all thought, logic, common sense and reasoning, not a reason to believe that God has the answers? Don't you believe God has the answers to even the most bewildering and mysterious questions that the mind of man cannot conceive? You, yourself have said that the finite mind of man cannot comprehend the infinite mind of God. Your vow of obedience is to trust that God will do what is right. It is not for you or the position of our order or its purpose to question God as to what has been done, or what continues to be done, or what will be done in the future. Gabriel, I know that it is not easy to be obedient when all around you are the temptations that cause you to question your faith and belief in God, and most of all your belief in Christ."

Gabriel could no longer contain his wrath and could no longer contain the bile in his throat nor the frustration and anger that consumed him, as he blurted out to Father Jacob words that Gabriel would one day regret. "I want God to hear my prayers. I want Him to answer me and show me that not only are my prayers heard, but those of the millions that pray to God each day. But more than anything, I want God to do something about fighting evil and defeating evil for mankind."

"I know Gabriel, you took the vow of humility and vowed to humble yourself before God and to forsake all others and yourself in servitude to the Lord. Do you not believe that others before you have sought the conclusive confirmation you seek. Oh, how easy it would be to be faithful to the Lord if He walked among us as He once did and allowed each of us to touch His wounds and, as a doubting Thomas, place our hand into the Lord's side. No Gabriel, faith and belief in God is not that easy a task, when we have but the word of God of what once was and again will be when Christ returns. Did He not say that He is the way and through Him you will meet the Father?"

"Father Jacob, I know all you say, but I did not come into this vocation to prepare myself for meeting my maker. I came here to forge a union with God to help eradicate evil and make the world a place where good triumphs over evil. That, Father Jacob, and nothing else is my vocation, but I need God to hear me and speak to me as to how I can help to make this happen."

Father Jacob, upon hearing Gabriel, said in a stern, clear, yet unyielding tone, "Gabriel, you are not Jesus Christ, and you are most certainly not God the Father. If you persist in this prideful manner, I have no alternative but to ask you to give up your vows and leave our monastery. But for now, I'm going to allow you to take a three month leave away from us and go out into the world to see if there is a path in your life that will allow you to make peace with God, to find out who you are, and what it is you are to do with your life."

"If you feel that is what is best, then I will do as you ask," replied Gabriel.

"I'm asking you to leave in the morning and you will be provided a sum of money for your use while you are gone. I hope that when you return, you will be ready to rededicate yourself in our monastic way of life. If you chose to do otherwise, you go with our blessing and our love as we all pray you will find the peace you seek. Now go and may God be with you."

"Thank you Father." Gabriel rose from his chair and knew there was nothing left to say. He was a lost soul who needed to find his way.

Chapter Two

Early the next morning, Gabriel decided to visit his brother Daniel, a parish priest in one of Milwaukee's older inner city parishes whose ethnic and racial makeup had changed over the past fifty years. He knew that Daniel would understand him and help guide him to make some sense out of the feelings and thoughts that had created these doubts and concerns over his vocation. His brother Daniel, and especially his sister Theresa, seemed so at peace with their life and chosen path. He needed to know and understand what was it that brought them the serenity in their lives he'd yet to find. Was God hearing their prayers? How did they reconcile the secular and worldly conflicts pulling humanity apart, and yet accept their role in the spiritual realm of their vocation? He knew they would listen and both would talk with him, and unlike Father Jacob, they would understand.

As he entered the sacristy, he could not help but notice the magnificent detail and splendor of this old cathedral whose years had yet to diminish the solemnity of this almost sacred structure. There, he was greeted by Father Daniel with a warm embrace. "Gabriel, Gabriel you are a welcome sight for these tired old eyes. What brings you to visit your big brother?"

"Big brother my eye, I'm still a head taller than you'll ever be, older yes, but bigger brother, not in my lifetime," joked Gabriel.

"I see that the monks haven't put any humility between those big shoulders or pinned those big ears back yet, but I'm confident and I'll guarantee they will very soon," replied Daniel.

"You can still see right through me, can't you," Gabriel said in a somber tone.

But Father Daniel was still sharing in the joy of seeing his brother and joked, "I had your number from the first day you were born, but you had mom and dad eating out of your hand. You and I always had a connection, though not as much as you have with Theresa, as you are and always have been the favorite of her two big brothers."

"That connection is why I'm here, and why I'm going to visit Theresa as well in the hopes that you both can help me."

"Yes, but come." directed Daniel, "Let me first get you something to eat and you can tell me how I can help."

Two hours later, Gabriel had shared his conversation with Father Jacob as to his failings in obedience and humility, and the challenges with his abiding faith and spiritual connection with the Lord. Listening intently to what Gabriel had just said, Father Daniel spoke in an equally serious tone.

"Gabriel, I love you with my whole heart and soul, and I've been very proud of you as are mom, dad, and Theresa. You have always been the best of us and I know of your deep convictions and the righteousness of your beliefs, but I believe you have come to a crossroads in your life. I believe that deep within you is the answer you seek. I can't say that the Lord won't speak to you directly, nor can I say that the Lord won't show himself directly to you. Too many of us, especially in our religious orders, would deny that which they feel is an entitlement of theirs for the life they've chosen. Yet, we know God moves in mysterious ways, as has happened with some of the many miracles we've seen. The visions of our Holy Mother appearing to children in numerous places around the world touched those that are the poorest among us. With God all things are possible. I know you are not asking to be an avenging angel acting as the hand of God yourself, but you are merely asking to understand why God isn't responding to the evil all around us. Struggling with that question should not have you questioning the very foundation of your faith," Daniel outlined.

"Dan, Theresa is really the best of us as she has always had a special relationship with the Lord. I'm hoping that when I visit with her, she can make some sense of my...," Gabriel paused as the words he wanted to say could not be formed. He began again to speak, only to again lose his ability to verbalize his feelings. Finally, Gabriel summoned the strength and courage to voice his thoughts. "Daniel, what am I to do with my life and not throw it all away? Yes, you're right I am at a crossroads in my life and faith."

Father Daniel responded, "I have no doubt that Theresa may truly be the one best able to give you some sense of it all or at least some direction if anybody can. You should visit mom and dad, I know they love you and want what's best for you as well."

With that said, the brothers again embraced as Daniel gripped his brother tightly to him and whispered, "Our Lord loves you Gabriel, give Him a chance to show you how much."

"Thank you Dan, thanks for listening, and thanks for your comments. They've helped me more than you know."

"Please give Theresa my love and please stay in touch and see mom and dad so they won't worry." As Daniel bid him good bye, Gabriel planned on visiting his parents in Chicago after visiting Theresa to let them know what was happening. But first, he wanted to come to some decision as to how he would pursue the rest of his life, so he could assure them everything was going to be all right.

At the knock on the door, the Mother Superior called to Theresa to enter her office, "Yes please come in, Sister Mary Theresa."

"Yes Mother, you asked to see me?" asked Theresa.

"Our affiliate in Milwaukee, St. Peter's parish where your brother, Father Daniel serves as pastor, needs someone to train a new Sister who has taken on similar duties as your own. They would like you to impart some of your administrative and inter-personal skills to assist her in her new role. You leave after services this afternoon and you will spend the next four weeks there. Sister Mary Catherine, who has helped you on occasion here, is fully conversant in your duties and will assume them in your absence. The Mother Superior, Sister Mary Beatrice will expect you around eight p.m. and she has made all the arrangements for your extended visit."

"Thank you Mother Superior, I will try to do my very best and will miss all of you here and I will look forward to my return."

"Thank you Sister Mary Theresa, we know you will do us proud and we will miss you and pray for a safe journey and a safe return."

Sister Mary Theresa wore simple and modest clothes that allowed her to blend into the general populace with little hint or display of her vocation other than the small cross she wore on a chain around her neck in plain view. She boarded the bus to Milwaukee on what she viewed as a welcome break in her routine and the opportunity to help others. It was well after eight in the evening when Theresa arrived at the convent that also contained the grade and middle school for the children in the area. She was immediately ushered into Sister Mary Beatrice's office and was soon joined by another nun about the same age as herself.

Without any sense of warmth or friendly greeting, the Mother Superior introduced herself and Sister Mary Magdalena. Mother Superior was all business and she seemed to address Sister Mary Magdalena with a lack of warmth and compassion. She quickly outlined the duties and tasks that Sister Mary Magdalena was to learn and proceeded to rattle off the accommodations, rules, and schedule that Theresa was to adhere to while there. Theresa as usual was attentive, obedient, and displayed a confidence that she was up to the task and at the same time greeted Sister Mary Magdalena with a smile to show her she was approachable and friendly.

Several days later after her arrival, she was summoned to the Mother Superior's office and upon entering saw Gabriel standing there with a warm smile on his face. Though joyfully surprised, Theresa decided to maintain a proper and professional demeanor in front of the Mother Superior rather than to run to Gabriel and throw her arms around him.

In her usual cold and serious manner, the Mother Superior seemed reluctant to allow Gabriel and Theresa a moment alone, as if suspecting Gabriel was other than Theresa's older brother. Luckily, Gabriel with his usual charm and forthright manner indicated that he had a grave family matter to discuss with Theresa and needed some time and privacy to talk with her. Dressed in his full religious garb, Gabriel helped resolve the Mother Superior's uncooperative spirit in acquiescing to Gabriel as a concerned brother. The fact that Father Daniel had also requested that Gabriel be allowed to visit with Theresa on an important Bonaci family matter seemed to resolve the Mother Superior's concern as to allowing the visit.

As the door closed behind the Mother Superior as she exited, Theresa asked, "How are mother and father?"

Gabriel quickly picked up on Theresa's ploy and waited until the door was fully closed before replying, "I'm going to stop and see them later this week. Daniel sends his love, but I came here to ask for your help." Gabriel again detailed the conversations he had had with Father Jacob as well as the one he had with Daniel and added his own additional frustrations, apprehensions, and concerns as to the direction his life had taken.

Theresa was supportive as Daniel had been, but she knew Gabriel better than the rest of the family, so she decided that tough love was what was required. "Gabriel, I do not see you, nor frankly did I ever see you, as a monk leading a monastic life. I see you more as a pastor of your own flock in which you are directing families in leadership of a Christian life. Today, families are struggling with dealing with the world as it is and need your guidance, support, and blessings in facing the challenges they will encounter in their lives. I see you, with all your talents and abilities, rising within the church to Monsignor, Bishop, Archbishop, and Cardinal. I see you increasing your good influence over a greater and greater number of the faithful," she said solemnly. "You could be our Holy Father, the Pope one day. I know you could, as God has a plan for you, but you seem so busy wanting God to hear you, you've closed yourself off to listening to Him and asking, as a servant of the Lord, what His expectations for you should be."

Theresa was always able to put things in a manner that Gabriel knew to be sound thinking and gave him little reason to disagree.

"Leave it to you to tell me what I needed to hear. I just haven't thought about it in those terms, but I'm not so sure about all that stuff of being a Bishop, Cardinal, or Pope kind of thing," Gabriel replied.

"Gabriel, you should start thinking in those terms and put your life in God's hands and go with the flow. God could sure use your help and our Church needs a leader like you and Christians all over the world are searching for someone who will fight the good fight and take up their cause. You can do it, I know you can."

Suddenly there was a knock at the door and the voice of the Mother Superior could clearly be heard asking if they were done talking as Theresa needed to finish her duties for the day. Theresa quickly hugged Gabriel and whispered in his ear, "You know Gabriel, you're my hero, now go out into the world and become theirs." As they broke their embrace, Gabriel called out, "Please come in Mother Superior." Gabriel extended his hand and thanked the Mother Superior as she clasped his hand in hers and said, "Go with God, Brother Gabriel."

Gabriel left the convent with much to think about. Theresa had been candid in telling him to listen to God and place himself in God's hands, open to anything that was to come. The idea that the religious life did not necessarily mean being a monk in the monastic traditions, but rather being a priest and pastor leading his own congregation had merit. In his motel room in Milwaukee that night, Gabriel prayed to God and asked God to give him clarity as to what Christ wanted him to do.

Within days after Gabriel's visit with his parents, Father Jacob called him indicating that the Cardinal of the Chicago Archdiocese, Cardinal Alberto Roncalli was in need of an administrative liaison. The Cardinal had heard about Gabriel and was inquiring as to whether he might have an interest in serving God in this capacity. Father Jacob convinced Gabriel that this might be the opportunity that he sought as an indication that God was reaching out to him as a sign of what God wanted him to do with his life.

The words of his sister Theresa suggesting that Gabriel could serve God within the community while still in a religious capacity echoed in his mind. This might indeed be an answer to his prayers. He responded to Father Jacob in a positive manner and thanked him for this opportunity.

Father Jacob replied, "Gabriel, I would love to take credit for bringing this matter to Cardinal Roncalli's attention, but you can thank your mother when you see her, as I'm told she did a real sales job on the Cardinal. I was only too happy to confirm to the Cardinal that all the things your mother had said were true and that you have my blessings to pursue this opportunity. An appointment has been made for you to meet with Cardinal Roncalli at his office this coming Thursday at ten in the morning. Gabriel, God bless you and go in peace."

Gabriel thanked Father Jacob for his blessing and asked for his forgiveness in his failure as a monk.

Gabriel immediately did some research on Cardinal Roncalli and found him to be a man in his mid-fifties who had been ordained as a Prince of the Church just two years earlier at the enclave that named the new Pope. He was a man noted to be outspoken in his defense of the church but was a modern theologian seeking to reconcile the modern world with the ancient traditions. He felt that the Church clung to too much pomp and circumstance surrounding the Holy See and wanted the faithful to see the church leadership live a life of simplicity that Christ had shown as an example while here on Earth.

He found that Cardinal Roncalli moved easily through the political entrapments of Chicago's secular community while maintaining a steadfast commitment to the teachings of the Church. The Cardinal was a friend to many whose wealth and power controlled the city and whose influence stretched to Washington D.C. at a national level. At the time of his appointment, many within the Church were surprised by his elevation from Archbishop of Milwaukee, as they did not see him as the pious pastor they had wanted him to be.

At more than six feet tall, slim and erect, Cardinal Roncalli came from a humble Italian heritage from the same neighborhoods that he now oversaw. He had many of the same attributes as Gabriel with a youthful exuberance, a keen intellect, and was blessed with a fair amount of charm in his own right. Gabriel's research revealed that the Cardinal was a law and order Bishop and later an Archbishop that aligned himself with intolerance of those who chose to violate the peace and tranquility of a well-ordered society. He seemed to be everything that Gabriel had read and imagined him to be when they met. He was strong in stature, quick on his feet with a friendly manner, and had a warm smile and an infectious laugh. It was said, he was not as pious as some had wanted him to be for someone who was to walk in the shadow of the Lord. No, here was a man who cast his own shadow and Gabriel liked him immediately and hoped that the Cardinal would have a similar impression of him.

"First of all Brother Gabriel, please do not address me as your eminence but rather when we are alone, I prefer Father Roncalli. You and I will be working together twenty-four seven and often you will wish that you had never agreed to be my assistant. Handling the public relations of this office is a full-time job. I will be creating enough controversy with our friends and enemies of this office that should keep you busy into the late hours of each day to make you yearn for the peace of your former monastic life."

"But your Eminence, you act as if I've accepted the position. Shouldn't we be sure that this is right for the both of us before we venture forth?"

"Gabriel, why waste my time. I've researched your background and I feel I know a great deal about you and your family. I have already had the opportunity to speak to your brother Daniel, your sister Theresa, and your father as well. You know that your mother already threatened me with bodily harm if I didn't offer you this position, so what's the holdup. You have an outstanding biography as a scholar, war hero, and athlete. Father Jacob gives you his thumbs up. I know you've checked me out, so as they say in the Corps, 'there's the hill - take the hill!' So, give me a yes and quit wasting more of my time. You've got sixty seconds and the clock is ticking, fifty-nine seconds and counting."

"Yes, I'll take the position before you change your mind."

"Now Gabriel, I'm going to have to give you one of those fancy titles to satisfy all those self-centered, pompous, and impervious people you'll come in contact with representing me and this office. Unfortunately, Brother Gabriel won't do, so you're to be called Monsignor Bonaci, and I hope the media doesn't make too much of our mutual Italian heritage or any mafia reference. I believe you to have the same thick skin as I do, so what they say about us, or the names we are called, is of little consequence. So Monsignor, are you prepared to do battle in the name of the Lord, and are you prepared to lead the army of souls to wage war to the very gates of hell?"As the Cardinal spoke, Gabriel sat in awe and whispered a silent prayer thanking God for hearing him and promising to never doubt God's plan for him ever again.

Gabriel's move to Chicago quickly threw him into the busy life of the Holy See. Life became as fast paced and as exciting as he would have imagined in corporate America. Only now, the corporation was the Holy Roman Catholic Church. Cardinal Roncalli was true to his word and reputation as Gabriel was thrown into every facet of the Cardinal's causes. The Cardinal was very pro-life, and he condemned the pedophilia within the church. He urged charity and charitable works, and he was also anti-crime, pro-law enforcement, and anti-drugs. He was a shepherd of the poor and those who were hungry, homeless and less fortunate. He hated abuse of power, corruption, and deceit. He spoke from the bully pulpit in every Catholic Church around the city. He led marches and spoke before many groups for this cause or that cause and did so speaking fluent Spanish, Polish, and of course, Italian. He galvanized the masses to mobilize them to each of his righteous crusades. He formed alliances among the Jewish, Greek Orthodox, as well as the Christian and Evangelical communities.

He even met with the Orthodox Islamic leaders in the community for the cause of peace. He was more popular than the mayor, and some even said that he was more powerful. He became a crusader for better living conditions, and showed little tolerance of those able to work but unwilling to do so in support of their families, especially their children.

In the mist of it all, was Monsignor Bonaci helping to orchestrate 'The Hand of God' as people in the city were beginning to call Cardinal Roncalli. Gabriel felt empowered that he had been given a true mission in life. He was in awe of the Cardinal and believed that one day Cardinal Roncalli would sit in Rome as the head of the church. Gabriel worked tirelessly, rising early and ending his day late at night. He too, was gaining stature in the city due to his proximate role in service to the Cardinal as many saw the loyalty and unity that Gabriel brought to the Cardinal's office. He had become known for his passion, dedication, and commitment to get things done no matter how large or small and no matter who asked or who objected. Some that became upset with Gabriel or his approach would complain to Cardinal Roncalli. They would be rebuffed in their objections and would find that the Cardinal was even more supportive of Gabriel's efforts to do what was right.

Both of Gabriel's parents were very proud of him and they had become celebrities in their own right among their fellow parishioners who often asked them to intercede with Gabriel on their behalf. But, none were prouder of Gabriel than his brother Daniel and his sister Theresa as both filled Gabriel's heart and spirit with a sense of accomplishment for what he had done with his life.

Chapter Three

Sister Mary Theresa missed her Abby at Holy Hill, Wisconsin, so on occasion she would contact them during her absence while at St. Peter's. Though she wanted to return soon, she knew her obedience and desire to fulfill her obligation at St. Peter's was more important. She felt that her work there among some the poorest parishes in the city was a blessing, though at times, she felt that poverty and poor living conditions had contributed to the crime and lawless nature among some of those she served. Then one day, returning from delivering food and clothing to a homeless shelter, she and Sister Mary Magdalena, a nun the same age as Theresa, became lost returning to the parish. As they ventured down some streets to gain their bearings, they came upon a group of youths and asked for directions.

One of the four male youths in the group, seeing Sister Mary Magdalena in the full religious garb of a nun's habit, responded by saying, "You two seem to be out of place in this neighborhood." But, before they could reply, one of the four girls in the group spoke up. "I think they're from that convent school at St. Peter's Catholic Church. That one is wearing the same kind of uniform."

Theresa again, in a polite but clear voice asked, "I would really appreciate it, if you could please direct us to St. Peter's Church, we've become lost."

Another of the male youths said sarcastically, "Are you sure you're lost or just looking to see how the other half lives and want in on some of our action?"

"Na," another youth replied, "I just think they're scared shitless, probably have never met the likes of us before and they're worried we're gonna put a world of hurt on 'em."

Another jumped into the conversation with, "Maybe they'd like to join our group."

Another laughed, "Hell, why would they want to hang around with the likes of us, they probably think they're too good for our kind and too high and mighty to want a share in any of our stash."

Theresa again stated, "We are nuns from St. Peter's Church and we just want to return there with your help, can you show us the way?"

"See, see, I told you," said one of the girls, "these are two nuns from the convent who were working at the shelter. Leave them alone and let them be on their way. Sisters, if you turn right at the next street," but before she could continue, she was shouted down by one of the older teen boys.

"Whoa, who made you the official guide, we don't get many like them coming into our hood and these two look like they could provide some of us with some enjoyable entertainment, that's what I think!"

Another of the girls in their group replied, "Wait a minute, I'm not having any of this and if you all know what's good for you, you'll leave them alone and let them be on their way." Within seconds, the girls backed away with some the boys muttering to each other, "Yeh, let's get outta here before we're sorry."

The girls and some of the boys disappeared around the corner leaving Sister Mary Theresa and Sister Mary Magdalena still surrounded by four of the remaining male teens.

Theresa spoke up again, "We are Sisters of Mercy and we were helping at the shelter and we are returning to our convent for the night."

"Well, at least one of them can talk," said one of the boys. "What about the one in the penguin suit, can she talk? If you're both sisters how come you're dressed different? Why aren't you wearing one of those penguin outfits or black robe get-ups like she does?"

Addressing their question, Theresa replied, "We are of different orders, mine allows us to represent our willingness to not want to stand out apart from those we serve in the community."

"Let me get this straight," said the older youth, "you think you blend in with us with what you got on. Well yah, you don't look like one of those black-dressed penguins like your friend here that's hiding her body so you only see her face and hands. Well, we can see your body pretty good and it doesn't look all that bad. So are you a virgin too, or just the ones with the black robes?" the youth continued.

"The sisters at the catholic school all wear what are called habits, and we all take a vow of chastity as we become brides of our Lord Jesus Christ," replied Theresa.

"So all of you are married to this same dude and doesn't that make Him one of those, what do you call them, a big something, yah that's it, a bigamist. But, none of you ever do it with this dude so you're all still virgins, right?" asked one of the other youths.

Theresa chose to ignore their comments and said in a sterner voice, "If you're not going to help us, we'll be on our way before we miss our bus back to the convent. So, we'll find our way back on our own if you don't mind, but thank you for your kindness."

"Well, you just listen to her royal highness, 'thank you for your kindness,' " he mimicked. "Who the hell do you think you're talking to? I'm no prince charming. What I'd like to do is get a look of what's under that long shirt you're wearing," the older youth threatened Theresa.

"Please," said Theresa in a louder voice, "we are asking you to leave us alone and let us pass, please," she repeated.

"I don't think so little sister," as one of the youths grabbed Sister Theresa from the rear and held both of her arms behind her and another youth did the same with Sister Magdalena.

Theresa spoke in a calm and clear voice betraying the fear she now felt for both herself as well as Sister Magdalena, "You do not want to be doing this as the Lord our God will protect us. Now release us immediately or the Hand of God will bring his wrath down on all of you!"

"Whoa," said one of the youths, "are we suppose to be scared or something, the 'Hand of God,' boy, I'm so frightened!"

No sooner had he finished speaking when the sky became very dark, the wind picked up, and thunder claps of deafening sounds caused the air to vibrate and the ground to shake. A brilliant flash of light against the darkening sky grew into a glowing globe of steady radiance. There, within the globe, the light became concentrated and the figure of an angel appeared holding a sword and carrying a shield. The vision now occupied a huge portion of the sky. The four youths, as well as Sister Theresa and Sister Magdalena, stood transfixed by the vision as they all stood in a trance as the angel pointed its sword toward the youths. From the tip of the sword emanated a laser beam of a blinding light that directed itself to just above the heads of the four youths. An explosion of sound caused the youths to collapse to the ground with their arms and legs shaking as if in a state of seizure.

Both Sister Theresa and Sister Magdalena knelt in awe of the vision and put their hands together in prayer as they remained unharmed. As suddenly as the vision appeared, the darkness subsided, the wind calmed, and the thunder ceased as the sky returned to a normal late afternoon setting.

Sister Theresa rushed to where the youths had fallen to the ground and though the seizures in each had subsided, they now lay unconscious as sirens could be heard in the near distance as fire trucks, ambulances and emergency vehicles all descended on the intersection. Also within minutes, media trucks and other vehicles poured into the area as the medical personnel began ministering to the youths as their pallor and breathing returned to normal. The police cordoned off the area as crowds began to gather to form a circle around the intersection. The youths were loaded into the EMT vehicles and the nuns were placed in police cars for their protection as T.V. and news groups clamored to talk to anyone who claimed to have seen and experienced the sighting of the vision that had just occurred.

It soon became apparent that the vision had been seen from miles away in all directions from the intersection. The media began contacting clergy of all denominations and conducting interviews as T.V. stations broke into their regular programming to bring on-site reporting as to what had occurred. Word spread quickly through phones and the internet as Twitter, Facebook, and blogs, and other media sources expanded to nationwide and worldwide coverage of the occurrence.

Archbishop Sullivan of Milwaukee, learning of the involvement of Sister Mary Theresa and Sister Mary Magdalena, quickly dispatched a church representative to the police station where they had been brought from the scene. Cardinal Roncalli, who had been quickly contacted, summoned Monsignor Gabriel Bonaci, together with a church attorney, to go immediately to the police station to bring both nuns to the convent in Holy Hill, Wisconsin. There they could be sheltered from the press and others outside of the church. It was obvious to Cardinal Roncalli this entire matter needed to be reeled in before hysteria followed, and the incident was blown all out of proportion.

As Gabriel entered the Cardinal's office, the Cardinal wasted little time in explaining to Gabriel specifically what needed to be done in Milwaukee. "Gabriel, I appreciate that Sister Mary Theresa is your sister, and one of the reasons you are being sent is to comfort her as someone she trusts. But, I am expecting you will be able to garnish the truth of what occurred, how it occurred, and separate the faithful true aspects of what occurred from the distortions that are surely to be fabricated by some. You are to report directly to me, assist the Archbishop, and ensure that Sister Mary Magdalena is afforded the same treatment as your sister."

"Both are not to speak to the media or anyone else and you will be present for both of them when they are lawfully required by law enforcement to give their statements as to what occurred. But, you will first meet with them before they give any statements to be sure that what they say is not manipulated. The Mother Superior at the convent, where they will be cloistered, is to give only you and no one else access to them without your permission. We must quickly establish the Church's position as to what occurred and did not occur before we release any official position regarding the vision or sighting. Though you will be given an attorney to handle any legal obstacles that might arise, you and you alone are the attorney for both nuns to maintain client/attorney privilege. You will also be given the names of church investigators that will be part of your team that will talk to witnesses and others that may be persons of interest in this matter."

"You are to be present on behalf of the two nuns when the youths involved are questioned. I want you to hear their words directly from their mouths and not from some pre-prepared statement or other second-hand information. Gabriel, have I made myself clear as to what and how you are to proceed? This is a very important matter and I need you to be the right person for this task. Are you Gabriel, that right person?"

"Yes Father, I am that right person," responded Gabriel.

"Good," replied the Cardinal, "now go and God be with you my son."

"Thank you for your confidence in me for allowing me to be there for my sister." Gabriel knew that his brother Daniel, as well as his mother and father, would also be excluded from conversations with Theresa. He knew that he had to assure them that he would keep them informed as to how Theresa was faring without jeopardizing the investigation. He immediately left for Holy Hill and knew that this location had to be kept from the prying eyes of the media as they would attempt to turn the site into an all-night and all-day media circus.

Through Gabriel, the nuns chose not to bring charges against the youths as a way to gain the youths' attorney's cooperation for Gabriel to be present when the boys were questioned and released. The youths were declared to not have been harmed medically by their confrontation with the angelic vision and they agreed to not bring any charges against the nuns as well. The four youths became instant celebrities with the media, and found themselves on several talk shows with offers to tell their story for sums of money these youths had only dreamt of ever having in their lifetime.

Lawyers came out of the woodwork wanting to represent them in suing the Church for any wrong doing for the trauma they had experienced. Gabriel was able to also glean their agreement not to sue in exchange for dropping the charges of assault and kidnapping that could have been leveled against them by the nuns.

City officials and other governmental entities, the media, and thousands of witnesses all attested to the fact that they had seen the sight of a huge angel in the sky. Speculation began to be reported regarding all the similar and conflicting reports of the sighting. The Catholic Church came out with a statement that clarified that the Church was not prepared to acknowledge nor deny what the people had seen as a matter having any religious significance. A spokesperson for the Catholic Church further stated that they were undertaking an investigation to determine what had actually happened. The Church also stated that any report of an alleged angelic visitation is a serious matter. Any conclusion as to what occurred could not be ignored nor could the church rush to embrace what thousands had seen as a heavenly vision. Nor, could the incident be attributed to some scientific explanation or other natural phenomenon.

Other religious leaders were quick to respond in ensuring that it was well understood that angels were not the specific or sole purview of the Catholic Church. The existence of angels and their visitations had been well chronicled in both the New and the Old Testament of the Bible. The other religious leaders argued that all religions and religious leaders had a right to participate in the ongoing investigations and to be a part of knowing what had happened. They also made it clear they did not appreciate the cloak of secrecy surrounding the incident as related to the involvement of the nuns, and how the nuns were being isolated from being questioned by these other religious leaders.

Religious leaders outside the Catholic Church wanted to know more about these two nuns and why they had not been brought forth and questioned by the civil authorities and made available to them to question as to what they saw and heard. They felt there was a need for the nuns to refute or support the story of the four youths and what tens of thousands had seen and observed. One of the youths had told one media outlet that one of the nuns had threatened them that if they didn't leave her alone, she would bring the 'Hand of God' down on them and destroy them. Then out of nowhere, this angel appears and zaps them with its sword. These religious leaders wanted to know what kind of a person would think that they could bring down the wrath of God on someone, and then make it happen. Lawyers for the youths had been clamoring for the arrest of the nuns for bringing about an assault on them. The Milwaukee police were accused of taking orders from the Catholic Church and certain media outlets were demanding an investigation by the FBI and the Justice Department into the far-reaching dictates of the Catholic Church into civil, lay, and public matters.

As Gabriel drove to the Holy Hill convent in Wisconsin from Chicago, he could not help but dwell on the fact that he had been seeking, even demanding, that God answer his prayers. He prayed that God would show His presence in the world as a concerned Creator. Gabriel had so wanted God to intercede on behalf of good to combat evil and now this incident in Milwaukee occurs. Maybe God does move in strange ways and now God was in the midst of it all and Gabriel could hardly wait to see Theresa to learn more from her as to what had indeed happened.

Theresa and Magdalena had been basically cloistered within the confines of the convent and sheltered from any communication with the outside world and were prevented from speaking to anyone as well. Each had been separated from each other until separate formal interrogatories could be taken by Gabriel and the church attorney that accompanied him. The church was conducting its investigation of the religious significance of the event. They needed to determine what, if anything could be attributed to some heavenly apparition, visitation, intercession, or even an intervention by a heavenly body or host. Separately, Theresa and Magdalena were apprised of Gabriel's visit.

Within minutes after arriving at Holy Hill, Gabriel was ushered into an office in which he would visit with both Sister Theresa and Sister Magdalena. He was surprised to find Theresa alone and waiting for him. Theresa ran to Gabriel and hugged him warmly. "Thank you for coming. I was so happy to hear that it was you that Cardinal Roncalli had appointed to visit with me. Gabriel, I'm so proud of you, now you are Monsignor Father Gabriel Bonaci." Suddenly, there was a knock at the door and Gabriel opened it to see a nun in full habit regalia silently staring up at him. Theresa immediately asked Sister Magdalena to enter and quickly introduced her to Gabriel using his full title. Gabriel extended his hand and Sister Mary Magdalena tentatively reached out to place her small hand into the oversized grasp of his hand.

"Monsignor Bonaci, it is a pleasure to meet you," she replied in a quiet but self-assured manner.

"It would please me if the both of you would address me as Father Gabriel. I'm glad to be of help to you both. But, I'm afraid that the task that lies ahead for us is not going to be easy as this whole matter has created quite a stir among the laity, all religious faiths, and especially the Catholic Church. Thanks to modern communication technology, word has spread around the world and the two of you are at the focal point that all are looking to for answers to their many questions. Now the first question I need to ask you both," Father Gabriel continued, "do either of you mind if all of our conversations are recorded for the record?"

Both nuns responded in unison. "No Father we do not have any objection at all."

"Good." He turned on the voice recorder and repeated the question. Both nuns again said they had no objection to the recording of their conversations. "Also, I need a statement from each of you as to whether prior to this moment, since you left the police station, either of you have spoken to each other privately, or to anyone else other than Monsignor O'Grady regarding this matter."

Again, each of them stated separately in their own words that the matter of the incident in Milwaukee had not been discussed with anyone and that each had been cloistered separately since their arrival at the convent. This meeting with him was the first time that each had seen each other since their release. The nuns, without being given any further direction, gave their title and name before responding for the purpose of identification.

"To be sure that our conversations are kept strictly confidential, we want to establish a client/attorney relationship. This will ensure that your statements and those you gave to the police under the watchful eye of Monsignor O'Grady, acting as your counsel, remain confidential. Do both of you agree that Monsignor O'Grady and I be retained to act as your personal attorneys as well?"

Quickly, without hesitation, Theresa said in a clear voice, "I, Sister Mary Theresa, agree to retain both Monsignors Bonaci and O'Grady as my personal attorneys knowing that they both represent the Catholic Church in this matter of the incident in Milwaukee."

Gabriel then stated for the record, "Sister Mary Magdalena, do you know that Sister Mary Theresa is my sibling in that I am her natural brother by birth. I need to know that this relationship will not create in your mind a conflict of interest in your legal representation. Do you still wish to proceed to retain myself, Monsignor Gabriel Bonaci, in addition to Monsignor O'Grady as your personal attorneys?"

Magdalena responded, "I, Sister Mary Magdalena do hereby agree to have Monsignor Gabriel Bonaci and Monsignor O'Grady as my personal attorneys and hereby waive any concern or impediment to your representation of me of any possible or potential conflict of interest in your family relationship with Sister Mary Theresa Bonaci."

"Wow," exclaimed Gabriel, "I'm impressed."

Sister Magdalena laughed and said, "Two years of law school prior to entering the convent will do that to you."

"Before I meet with each of you separately, I must inform you that my concentration in this matter will be as your personal attorney ensuring that all of your rights are protected. Monsignor O'Grady's concentration will be ensuring that the rights of the Catholic Church in this matter will be protected. Should he ever ask you a question when I am not present in which you feel your rights are being violated or being infringed upon, you will merely advise him that you would like my presence before you respond with an answer."

Theresa spoke up, "I'm not as well versed in the law as Sister Mary Magdalena, as I'm not sure what exactly you're saying Father Gabriel."

Gabriel was expecting that clarification may need to be made regarding his most recent instruction and was prepared with the appropriate response. "You do not need to answer questions that have to do with you personally as to your preferences, opinions, and personal information regarding your past as they have no reflection on the incident in Milwaukee. Also, you do not need to share your interpretations of what may or may not have happened where you feel your religious beliefs may come into question. You are always free and able to respond to any question where you feel confident no such conflict exists. You then may proceed to answer the question as best you can."

"The bottom line as far as Monsignor O'Grady is concerned, is that he is representing the Church from an ecclesiastical position for the Holy Order of the Church. He will consider what you saw, heard, and said concerning the incident in Milwaukee. He will determine whether what occurred was a weather-related phenomenon, a freak incident of nature, or a vision. In representing the Church, he will determine whether or not if what you saw, and what thousands of others saw, was a viable visitation, intercession, or intervention. Do you both understand what the differences are between those theological beliefs that the Church holds?"

Theresa responded, "I believe we do, but please tell the both of us so we understand what Monsignor O'Grady is trying to determine."

A visitation is when the Angel Gabriel appeared to Joseph, the future husband of Mary, telling him that the Holy Spirit would come to Mary and that she would become the Mother of God and would give birth to the Son of God. Or, a visitation is when Mary appeared to the children of Guadalupe, Mexico and Lourdes in France. In these heavenly incidences, the appearance of the angel to Joseph, or Mary's appearance to the children, were not requested by either Joseph or the children. An intercession is when an earthly being requests the appearance of a heavenly being and the heavenly being intercedes on behalf of the earthly being to aid them. An example of this is when Moses called upon the wrath of God to intercede on behalf of the people of Israel. An intervention is when a heavenly being chooses to intervene into the natural order to bring about an action to change or alter that natural order. Certainly, the Holy Spirit that allowed Mary to become the Mother of God and give birth to the Son of God was a true intervention that had not been requested by Mary nor was it a mere visitation. Another example of an intervention is when the fallen angels came and had relations with humans to create the Nephilims in a causal relationship that would not have occurred in the natural order."

"Once science and atmospheric changes that are in the natural order of the universe are ruled out, Monsignor O'Grady will determine on behalf of the Church what really happened in Milwaukee. He will determine the vision as being a heavenly being and he will determine what caused the vision to occur. Do you now both understand? I, as your personal attorney will ensure your rights are not violated nor will you be coerced to say or deny anything unless that is what you want to say. I will not be with each of you individually when Monsignor O'Grady speaks with you. However, I will approve and verify that what you have said is written in your final statements of the investigation as your true words. Once each of you has given your statements, you will be allowed to return to your regular tasks and duties at your respective convents. But, each of you has been asked to give a vow of complete silence regarding anything pertaining to the incident in Milwaukee. Finally, after completing your separate interviews, those statements will be reviewed by me and

Monsignor O'Grady to determine if one of you said something the other did not. Or, if there are any conflicts or differences in each of your testimonies that may need to be reconciled. If there are conflicts that cannot be reconciled to the satisfaction of both myself and Monsignor O'Grady, a third church attorney will be appointed by the Cardinal who has the final decision in this matter as to what should be sent to our Holy Father in Rome. You will be allowed to appeal any such determination to the Holy See before they make a final determination."

Both of the nuns said in unison, "We understand and agree to comply with the terms and conditions you have set forth."

Theresa asked in a hesitate voice, "How are the boys, are they all right?"

"Other than to say they are all right, I can't say more at this time."

Chapter Four

News anchor, Brenda Copeland, stood on the corner in Milwaukee where the incident had occurred two days earlier. She was surrounded by the four young men involved and each seemed very anxious to tell their story before the national media. "So," began Ms. Copland to the camera, "is this the spot where you were standing and tell me what was taking place before you saw the appearance of an angel?"

"Yeah man," said one of the youths, "I was standing right here trying to give these two nuns some directions on how to get to their bus stop 'cause they didn't know where to go."

"Nah, that isn't when the angel appeared," said one of the other youths. "The one nun started walking in the wrong direction and when I grabbed her arm to, you know, sort of steer her in the right direction, she said something about the 'Hand of God' or something like that."

Another of the youths joined in, "Yeah for sure, she said the 'Hand of God', I heard her for sure that's what she said."

The first youth to whom Ms. Copeland had spoken to added, "Yeah, it was like she was threatening me for grabbing her arm when that's all I wanted to do was help her get home or wherever she was going, 'cause as soon as she said 'Hand of God', then this huge angel appears in the sky."

Ms. Copeland directed her mike at one of the youths that had yet to say anything. "Is that what happened and what did you see?"

"Did I see the angel? Hell, it was over one hundred feet tall and he had this huge sword that musta been twenty-five feet long, and he pointed it at us and then a bolt of lightning came out from the point straight at us and that's the last I remember."

Placing the mike in front of the last youth that had remained silent, Ms. Copeland asked, "Do you agree with what the others said and what they saw?"

Somewhat sheepishly, the youth responded, "No man, that isn't how it went down," and before he could say more, one of the boys yelled out, "Marcus shut your mouth. You don't know what you're talking about. If you know what's good for you, you'll keep your yap shut, if you know what I mean," he threatened.

"No Leroy," the boy retorted, "my momma said that God sent the angel to protect the nuns when you grabbed their arms and threatened to hurt them."

Copeland turned to one of the youths and asked, "Are all of you telling the truth, did any of your friends threaten the nuns?"

"No way man, why would we want to be threatening some nuns, not like they got anything we'd be wanting," said Leroy.

Another of the youths spoke up, "I guess them nuns just got scared being lost and all, and having four guys giving 'em some jive must've made 'em nervous. But, that angel sure did appear mighty fast after one of the nuns told us to leave them alone or the 'Hand of God' would get us."

Copeland looked into the camera as she turned toward Marcus and asked, "Marcus, how did you know that what you saw was an angel, and was it a man or women angel?"

"Geez man, I don't know, I didn't see any body parts or anything. He or she was carrying this big sword and had a big shield and I couldn't see the face real good because of the bright light shinning all around it. But, it had this big set of wings so I know it was some kind of an angel. My momma showed me pictures and this one could have been one of them archangels. My momma said it could have been like the angels Michael or Gabriel. I don't know if there are girl angels or not."

"Listen to you," Leroy butted in, "my momma this and my momma that. Your old lady is so drunk half the time that she probably sees angels all the time and what the hell difference does it make, boy/girl, it was one big ass angel that's for sure!"

"Well, thank you," concluded Ms. Copeland ending her interview and turning to speak to the camera.

"You have heard right here, from the very spot where it happened, from the boys to whom it happened. There is no mistake about it, they all saw an angel. We are receiving thousands of calls to our station and more than a thousand messages to our website from our viewers indicating they too saw an angel and these calls are coming in from all over the city. This is Brenda Copeland from WRPQ bringing you live coverage of the angel sighting in Milwaukee."

"Thank you Sister Mary Magdalena for allowing me to get your testimony recorded for the record," stated Gabriel. Sister Magdalena did not appear to be nervous and from the brief conversations in Theresa's presence, Gabriel was impressed with her articulate and confident manner. Her comment about law school led Gabriel to believe that this nun had been out in the world before she entered the convent and not as others who chose a religious order immediately out of an all-girl Catholic high school. Within an hour of questioning as to what she saw, heard, and felt about the incident in Milwaukee, Gabriel found her to be very intelligent, pragmatic, and forthright in her answers. She did not relate any fear as to her encounter with the youths nor did she seem in awe of the angelic sighting. Though Gabriel's experience with nuns was limited to his sister Theresa, he could not help but note she lacked a certain piety in her manner and wondered what had driven her to choose a religious vocation over one in the secular world. He was curious as to what her reaction would be to such questions as they might be seen as intrusive into her personal life, but he chose to ask anyway.

"Sister Magdalena, may I ask you what motivated you to choose a religious vocation after having gone to college and law school?"

"Yes Father Gabriel, both college and law school gave me the opportunity to see the secular world for what it was, a temporary profession within a temporal world of duties and challenges. It appeared to me that I would be struggling to make a contribution for a better world with little hope of changing the circumstances of the world that only seemed to be getting worse. There are few lasting solutions to the many problems in the world that need to be resolved. My ability and talents do not seem to lend themselves to efforts in finding cures for diseases, or feeding the millions that are hungry, or sheltering the millions that are homeless. It never ends! Since the dawn of time, people in the world have always been ravaged with disease, hunger, thirst, and homelessness. Even the good leaders of the world are powerless to bring about permanent solutions and are always combating the bad leaders of the world to right the wrongs that the bad leaders continue to perpetuate. Tell me Father Gabriel, what profession do you know of that within seventy or eighty years of your time on earth, will be able to end wars forever and find a lasting peace for all of mankind?"

Father Gabriel could not believe the words that had just come forth from this woman of no more than twenty-five years of age. He was hearing the same words that had tormented him as he was trying to make some sense of his life as well. "Sister Magdalena, you amaze me with the clarity of your thinking and reasoning, as well as the rational of your thoughts. I have had the same feelings as you have had and for the same reasons, I chose a religious vocation for myself. Tell me, did you ever think of marrying and having children as a vocation rather than becoming a nun?"

"Father, my parents had a horrible marriage as my father was abusive to my mother. Frankly, my mother was not much of a mother, as her whole life seemed to be trying to please my father in an effort to curb his abuse. Then finally, as my father's abuse turned on me and my two sisters, my mother divorced him. Then later, seeing my older sisters enter into equally devastating marriages with drugs, alcohol, cheating husbands, and neglected children, I realized that my temporal life on earth could be better spent in other ways. I began to focus on the eternal afterlife and how I might lead a life that would reap the rewards of a religious vocation."

"Sister Magdalena, though I can't begin to understand what you endured in your childhood and how it affected your thinking as to marriage and children, my parents today are as much in love with each other as they were almost forty years ago. I, my brother, and sister felt loved and cherished throughout our lives as our parents devoted themselves to our care and upbringing. But yet, today my sister is a nun, my brother is a priest, and me, well you know the outcome of that."

"Early on," Sister Mary Magdalena continued, "I thought I could

change my thinking how marriage and raising children would be like for me. I also thought I could learn from the mistakes of my parents and siblings. But, throughout college and law school as I dated, far too many of the men I met fell into categories that reminded me of my family situation with cheating boyfriends, and arrogant self-absorbed males. Frankly, I saw and met many very poor husband and father figures. The joys of nature and the beauty of God's creations soon took hold. I decided why not devote my life to serving the Creator, and serving the humans He created to help them overcome their earthly challenges. Finally Father, if we are finished with any further questions about the incident in Milwaukee, I did want to share something with you regarding Sister Mary Theresa as to how she has impacted my life in the brief time we've known each other, if that is permissible?"

"Only if what you are about to share is pertinent to the incident in Milwaukee and you agree to allow that conversation to be on the record, will I agree," concluded Gabriel.

"Yes, I believe that in the context of helping to determine what may have caused the appearance of the angel relevant to what you shared about visitation, intercessions, and interventions, it may be pertinent."

"If you feel that this may be the case, I will allow you to begin. But if I feel that it is not related to the Milwaukee incident, I suggest that we discuss the matter as privileged conversation between attorney and client and we can converse off the record if you wish to continue."

"Yes Father, I am agreeable to do that if that's what you decide."

"Sister Mary Theresa and I spoke at length about why I chose a religious vocation, similar to what you and I have just discussed. I asked her the reasons she had chosen a religious vocation and I was very intrigued by her reply. Her answer was not as logical and pragmatic as my reasons as she spoke of her love of Jesus. To her, He was a real flesh and blood presence in her life. To her, they were truly married as a husband and wife sharing in doing His work on Earth on behalf of the Father and caring for those less fortunate. When I questioned what she meant, being a bride of Christ, to her it was not in the ecclesiastical tenants of the Church as all nuns become the bride of Christ. She shared her love of Jesus and shared her feelings of being loved by Him in a very real way. She spoke of how she felt a radiance of love coarse through her body enveloping her in a way in which her mind felt His presence and she was with Him in a very real sense. Father, I was awed by her words, and I could tell that there was a sense of reality to what she was experiencing."

"Excuse me Sister Magdalena, but I'm not sure we are on a path that ties us to the incident in Milwaukee," questioned Gabriel. "But, I will allow you to continue on the record."

"She claims that when she prays to Him she can hear His voice responding to her questions. She says she hears His reassurances, forgiveness, and feels His joy in her discovery of the beautiful world the heavenly Father created. Above all else, it gives her comfort in His understanding of her concerns as to the evil in the world and for all the suffering that others have endured."

"Enough Sister Magdalena, I hear what you are saying, but I don't see the connection to the incident in Milwaukee and therefore I'm going to end this recorded conversation," concluded Gabriel.

"Wait Father, in my entire life, I have never met someone that when I'm with them I feel like I'm in the presence of a truly holy person and I feel nearer to God when I'm around Sister Mary Theresa."

"Thank you for sharing that," Gabriel hesitantly acknowledged.

Sister Mary Magdalena paused as though weighing whether to continue as she sought the right words to convey what she knew must be said. She then proceeded in a very reluctant manner. "Ok, this isn't going to be easy especially knowing you're her brother, but maybe because of that, it gives me the courage to say what needs to be said."

"Say what you please Sister Magdalena, what is it you want to say?"

"Father, I feel at peace when I'm with her, with an almost overwhelming calm and serenity in her presence. Like the time when those youths were harassing us and their words and actions were very frightening, I wasn't afraid. Sister Theresa displayed no nervousness, no anger, she just stood up to them all and I knew with her there I was safe and no harm would come to us."

"Sister Magdalena, though we are still on the record, and I appreciate and am touched by all you are saying, I must meet with Sister Theresa today to get her statement and we can meet at another time."

"Please hear me out Father, this is very important. One day she was in our chapel alone when Mother Superior sent me to find her and as I entered the chapel, I saw her kneeling before the crucifix of our Lord. As she prayed, she was unaware of my presence. There was an aura of light surrounding her silhouette that was almost a foot wide. It was like an energy field about her as she prayed. She somehow sensed my presence and the light diminished and extinguished as she turned to me and said, 'Are you looking for me?' This light was not coming through the windows nor was it a reflection from the sun off some other object; it was emanating from her. As her brother, you must have seen and experienced that light around her when she prays."

"I am unable to share with you, Sister Magdalena, off or on the record, my experiences or thoughts regarding Sister Mary Theresa regardless of the fact that I am her brother. I am not able to enter into these kinds of conversations or I may be required to seek other council for her," acknowledged Gabriel.

"Am I prohibited from sharing what I saw with Monsignor O'Grady when he meets with me for my statement?"

"No, I will not censure your comments from Monsignor O'Grady as he is your attorney as well and he will advise you if he feels that your comments should be on or off the record as I have in our conversation."

"But Father," Magdalena protested, "I thought you as her brother would understand and come to believe that Sister Mary Theresa did in fact summon the heavenly host to protect us and that you would believe this more readily than all others. I believe she has the ability to almost command a heavenly spirit to intercede on her behalf."

"What you say Sister Magdalena is a matter of conjecture on your part, and while I concur that Sister Mary Theresa walks in the grace of God, the Church will make the determination that she has achieved a level of oneness with our Lord that could give her such powers."

"No Father, I believe that she has a relationship to the Lord that is well beyond the realm of what anyone might feel possible. I feel the presence of the Holy Spirit when I am with her. Surely, both you and your family know what I mean. But, I only share this with you as her brother and will say nothing to anyone, other than Monsignor O'Grady about my feelings."

"Thank you Sister Mary Magdalena, I truly appreciate all the kind words and feelings you have for Sister Mary Theresa, but as your attorney, we should treat these kinds of conversations as off the record and as one of client/attorney privilege. If we have concluded your statement, I will summon Sister Theresa for her statement."

"Thank you Father, please do not say anything to Sister Theresa about what I've shared with you."

"No, you have my word on that," Gabriel assured her. "I know you must be exhausted after our session, but I'd like you to be available to meet with me again after I've gotten Sister Theresa's statement."

Meanwhile in Chicago, Cardinal Roncalli was being inundated with calls from all over the world wanting a clarification as to what had been reported and what official position the Church had taken regarding this incident. The Cardinal's response was that while the investigation was well underway, no conclusion had yet to be achieved. What was clear at this point was that while thousands of people had photographed the vision of the angel, the brilliant light emanating from the vision could not be recorded in any great detail. The pictures caught on film and digital imaging showed only shadows and outlines of the image. Therefore, only the testimony of eyewitnesses could be relied upon to verify that an apparition of an angel had occurred. There was also no tangible evidence or proof that anything at all had occurred as the four youths had received no visible injuries, nor were any marks left at the site, it was as if, it never had happened. Yet, the Church was plunged into the middle of this mania, because it was two nuns that were at the site with the four youths. There was nothing else to support the vision and the experience of thousands of others.

While Monsignor Bonaci was with the two nuns getting their statements, Monsignor O'Grady was delving into the backgrounds of the two nuns. He began with Sister Mary Magdalena by conducting interviews with members of her family, friends, neighbors, classmates, instructors and employers, as well as at her convent and parish where she served. He found nothing unusual about her. She was by all accounts very highly thought of by all. Some were surprised that she chose a religious vocation and chose to enter a convent. Some described her as popular, outgoing, friendly and highly intelligent but none spoke of her as deeply religious or pious in her demeanor. Her conduct was always above reproach and she was thought to be highly principled with no record or reports of any misconduct. Basically, she was a good girl from a somewhat dysfunctional family, who never did anything wrong or brought any negative attention to herself. But at the same time, she did not stand out as someone who was destined to be a nun. She used the name 'Maggie' as her given name all throughout her life until she entered the convent.

His investigation into Sister Mary Theresa drew a sharp contrast to that of Sister Mary Magdalena. Theresa was from a very early age an extremely pious child and all spoke of her goodness, caring and gentle nature. Her free hours were spent in prayer and doing good works even from a very early age. She cared for children, and ran errands for the elderly and infirmed. Later as a youth, she became an auxiliary member serving the church, cleaning the rectory, and assisting the nuns. She led programs for youths and helped the Altar and Rosary Society. Everyone spoke of her warmth, kindness, and loving nature.

It was the conversation he had with a priest who served the nuns in the convent by performing daily mass, hearing their confessions, and administering to their last rites as needed, that startled Monsignor O'Grady with what he had to say.

"I do not and will not betray the sanctity and confidentiality of the confessional," Father Hubert told Monsignor O'Grady. "But, I believe especially under the circumstances of your investigation regarding Sister Mary Theresa, you need to know and understand what I've experienced each time I have taken her confession."

"Nor will I ever ask you to do so," confirmed Monsignor O'Grady. "But any help you are able to give us in better understanding either of the nuns involved in the incident in Milwaukee would be of great benefit to us."

"Sister Mary Theresa is a nun whose confessions always have to do with her own feelings of inadequacy that she has not done enough to be worthy of the life she has been given. She questions whether her self-sacrifice is ever enough, or her love of God is ever sufficient. She feels anguish and deep torment for those less fortunate and cares for the plight of the hungry, homeless, ill or dying."

Monsignor O'Grady was moved time and time again as Father Hubert shared story after story of Theresa's feelings of failure, that she had not done enough in her daily life to help others in her devotion to Christ. It was as if, since Christ could not be among us at this time, she as His spiritual bride on Earth needed to go about her spouse's business.

"But Monsignor, it was nothing that she said that startled me, but what happened within the confessional that gave me pause to ponder as to what manner of a human being was in my confessional. As I would open the confessional partition to the screen that separates us, a glow of light seemed to be emanating from her side of the confessional. On one occasion, I asked if she had a flashlight with her and asked her to turn it off. Of course she denied it and was confused by my question, but as I gave her the blessing and her penance, the light illuminated to a brighter glow."

Monsignor O'Grady could not wait to meet this nun as she seemed to walk in the favor of God. The recent friendship that had developed between Monsignor Bonaci and himself had given no hint that Gabriel's sister might be a saint that had come amongst them. It seemed like out of nowhere, she had come to now be involved in one of the most significant religious incidents in over one hundred years. As he traveled to the convent in Holy Hill, Wisconsin, where the Basilica of Mary receives more than one-half million visitors each year, he wondered if it could be possible that there was a direct connection between this obscure nun and the vision seen in Milwaukee. When he arrived, he found that Gabriel was concluding his conversation with Sister Mary Magdalena in getting her statement and learned that he had yet to speak with Sister Mary Theresa. He decided that rather than meet with Sister Mary Theresa before she had spoken with Gabriel, he would wait to speak to Sister Mary Magdalena instead.

After meeting with Sister Mary Magdalena for more than two hours, Gabriel found her to be extremely detailed in her answers and yet organized in her thoughts and concise about the information she shared. It was obvious she was very intelligent and wanted to please him with her answers as she had an almost photographic memory of what had transpired with Sister Mary Theresa. She was factual, almost too precise in her words, of what each of the participants had uttered among the group of youths that confronted them that late afternoon.

Gabriel was surprised by some of her conversation regarding Sister Mary Theresa that Sister Mary Magdalena willingly shared. Before meeting with Theresa, he knew he wanted to replay her conversation with him, so he could retain and recall what she had said before meeting with Theresa. Her recall of the conversations with the youths was in conflict with what the youths had said to the media. Obviously, the youths had colored their version of the conversation so they did not appear to be the low-life street punks Sister Mary Magdalena had described them as being. In her version, they were threatening, intimidating, and sexually provocative in the nature and tone of their words, versus their version in which they purported their conduct as being helpful and respectful.

Gabriel could not help but replay Sister Mary Magdalena comments regarding his sister Theresa. He knew that she was special and he knew that she was a good person but the depth of her goodness as perceived by others was something that he never considered. They were probably closer than most brothers and sisters but he had no idea of what others had shared. The exchange of letters when he was in Afghanistan and Iraq had become a lifeline for him in dealing with the trauma of war and his loneliness away from the family. He knew there was a very strong and close bond between the two of them. But, never did he ever suspect Theresa to be the way Sister Magdalena and others had described her to be.

Chapter Five

Monsignor O'Grady arrived at Holy Hill a few days after having visited the Sisters of Charity in Milwaukee where Sister Mary Magdalena resided and served as a nun. In exploring the background of Sister Mary Magdalena, her fellow nuns had nothing extraordinary to share about her, but they also had nothing unusual to share as well. By all accounts, she was a good member of the order and was highly thought of as being obedient, penitent and hard working. She was also highly intelligent as she could quickly grasp certain tasks and served in various roles throughout the convent. She was considered by her Mother Superior to be trustworthy and a credit to the order.

Upon arriving at Holy Hill, and learning that Monsignor Bonaci was still in conference with Sister Mary Magdalena, Monsignor O'Grady decided to visit with other nuns to learn more about their impressions of the two nuns and gain information specifically on Sister Mary Theresa. Soon the revelations that were shared with him about Sister Theresa, known to them affectionately as the 'Little Flower,' startled him beyond all imagination. In one interview, a nun who had no particularly close connection with Sister Mary Theresa allegedly saw something that was beyond the realm of possibility. Surely she had to be mistaken or there was some other rational explanation as to what she encountered. He could not recall in recent times it ever happening to another. But yet, he heard the nun relate in a clear and concise manner that what she had seen was a revelation beyond human belief. He pressed her for clarification, asking her to repeat and reaffirm what she had seen. Yet she was unwavering in what she had witnessed. He asked if she had spoken to others of what she had observed or whether others had seen what she had experienced.

"I have only spoken to Mother Superior about this, and she told me to never speak to anyone about such a matter. But, I felt that speaking with you about this would be all right in light of the incident in Milwaukee and Sister Mary Theresa's involvement and the investigation you are conducting. I hope Father O'Grady, that in speaking to you, I have not broken my vows of silence as to what occurs within the confines of our convent. I am sure that if other nuns had shared my experience, they too would have gone to Mother Superior as well."

"Sister Mary Gertrude, why did you really break your vow of silence?"

"Monsignor, the world needs to know that we have a saint living among us and what happened in Milwaukee is proof of the love God has for her."

"Sister Gertrude, I too must request that you speak to no one about this, but I must speak with Mother Superior about this and I'm sorry that she will know from me that you have broken your vow of silence. I will tell her that you were correct in sharing this with me under the circumstances of my investigation." Monsignor O'Grady wasted little time in going directly to see the Mother Superior.

"Please Mother Superior," asked Monsignor O'Grady, "tell me what you know of Sister Gertrude's claim of her observations of Sister Mary Theresa. You know that I have a job to do here, and Cardinal Roncalli has set forth a mission that Monsignor Bonaci and I are to learn as much as possible about the two nuns that were involved in the Milwaukee incident for our investigation."

"Yes Monsignor, I am fully aware of the need for you to conduct your investigation, but I do not believe you have the right to invade the sanctity of our order and what goes on within these convent walls, or to assume that the world has any right to know what is contained herein."

"Please Mother Superior Immaculata, I do not wish to intrude into the life of your order nor do I expect you to allow the secular world to invade the holy confines of your convent. But, if what Sister Mary Gertrude tells me is correct, then we have a matter that needs to be brought to the Cardinal's immediate attention. The ramification, as to what happened in

Milwaukee, has a direct relationship with Sister Mary Theresa. I can only tell you that in my investigation, I have already gained from others that they too have had observations of Sister Mary Theresa in which a glow of light surrounds her during private prayer. If others have observed what Sister Gertrude has shared with me, and if that is true, you have within the walls of this convent an individual that is truly in the grace of God."

"Monsignor, I cannot confirm nor will I deny what you have heard or what you have been told, but I do feel that she is in the grace of God."

"Are you saying that you yourself have never witnessed the glow of light surrounding Sister Mary Theresa during prayer or witnessed her levitate. You know Mother Superior that you are under the direction of Cardinal Roncalli to share with me what you know, have seen, and what you have been told regarding Sister Mary Theresa. Especially in light of the investigation being conducted on the incident in Milwaukee, you surely understand the magnitude and purpose of my investigation and the authority I bring to this matter."

"Monsignor, you have made yourself perfectly clear as to the authority you believe you possess and the power from which it was granted to you. However, in my convent and in our order, I too am accountable to a higher authority. You will need to seek his permission for me to share what transpires within the walls of this convent and what concerns the nuns that make up our order," retorted the Mother Superior.

"And who," Monsignor O'Grady interjected, "has higher authority than Cardinal Roncalli?"

In a more compliant tone, Sister Mary Immaculata responded, "Please check with the papal authority in Rome and you will find that the charter granted our order more than two hundred years ago does not place us under the Cardinal's jurisdiction. Sister Gertrude is free to speak her mind and what she shared with you was of her own free will to do so, but please do not assume you can order or demand others within these walls, including myself, to be forced into sharing anything we choose not to share. I hope I have now made myself infinitely clear."

"Yes, you have made yourself infinitely clear. But, under the circumstances I do not believe your position is attainable within the confines of this investigation. I hope that I and Monsignor Bonaci are still free to speak to others, as well as Sister Mary Theresa, in the course of this investigation. I assume you want to allow others, as you have stated, the free will to say what they want to say. Mother Superior, I mean you no harm or any of the other nuns within the confines of this convent and I will do all I can to protect the privacy of your sanctuary. What I find out in this investigation is solely for Cardinal Roncalli's eyes and his alone. Unfortunately, your nuns and your order are in the middle of it all. The Church has a responsibility to ensure that we do not have mass hysteria. The Church, within the confines of this vision that has been seen by thousands, must be able to clarify what occurred, and whether or not there is any religious significance to its occurrence."

"Yes, I understand," concluded the Mother Superior, "you have a very important and very difficult task. But, once you've spoken to Sister Mary Theresa, I am confident that you will conclude that there is no connection between her and this incident in Milwaukee. The fact that we may have among us an individual who may be on her way to sainthood, can then remain within the confines of these walls until another day."

Monsignor O'Grady understood that he was not going to be able to see Sister Mary Theresa until Monsignor Bonaci had secured her testimony. So the next morning, he set out to speak with some of the other nuns that may have come in contact with Sister Theresa during a time she was engaged in prayer. Surely others had seen the glow of light surrounding her or better still, they may have observed her in levitation. My God, he thought, to have one among us that has been given the gift to defy the laws of science and nature is a miracle in of itself. He thought of Father Cupertino, who not only levitated but had the stigmata of Christ where the wounds in his hands would bleed in prayer. He was a true mystic and saint and could it be possible that this Sister Mary Theresa was another like him in our place and time.

Although Mother Superior Immaculata refused to confirm or deny what Sister Mary Gertrude had said, she in fact had observed not only the glow of light but Theresa's levitation as well. She knew the full implication of what she had seen when coupled with the heavenly vision in Milwaukee that gave credence to the fact that one of God's hosts had come in response to Sister Mary Theresa's plight. She was convinced that a heavenly host had interceded on Theresa's behalf in a most direct, yet unusual manner.

The need within Monsignor O'Grady and the building anticipation to meet with Sister Mary Theresa had now created such a sense of urgency that he was not able to sleep for most of the night. He awoke with a burning desire to escalate and expand on his investigation and was now most anxious to meet with Monsignor Bonaci to learn more of how his interviews may have gone. He knew that once he was able to lay out all of the information he had gleaned and present that to Cardinal Roncalli, the very foundations of St. Peters Basilica in Rome and the Holy Father himself would be shaken to the core.

"Thank you for coming, Sister Mary Theresa," Gabriel officially welcomed her into the room, signaling that their meeting was to be officially between attorney and client.

Theresa, though wanting to address Gabriel by his by his given name, but suspecting that the recorder and video tape might be on, greeted him likewise with the formal, "Good morning Monsignor Bonaci." But, she quickly learned that they were off the record and she asked, "Gabriel, I do have something I want to say."

"Absolutely Theresa, what is it you want to say."

"Thank you Gabriel, at this moment I'm not talking to you as Sister Theresa to Monsignor Bonaci, I'm talking as Theresa your little sister speaking with her big brother, is that ok?"

"Theresa, are you going to get after me for something I've done wrong? Ok, go for it, what have I done now," sighed Gabriel.

"Oh Gabriel, you haven't done anything wrong, you've done so much right that it makes me so proud of you. You've done so much since becoming a Monsignor and senior aid to Cardinal Roncalli. I hear all about the good works that you've got the archdiocese doing for the poor, homeless, and the less fortunate, especially the children. You are in my prayers each night and I ask God to continue to bless you in all you do. You were always my hero, but now you are a hero to millions that praise the church because of your efforts." As quickly as she began, she concluded with, "Ok that's it, I don't want you getting a big head, but I do know that God loves you as well."

"Theresa," interjected Gabriel, "let me ask you a question before we begin your testimony and I want you to be completely honest with me."

"Gabriel you know that's the only way I know how to be. What is it, what is the matter, is something wrong?" pleaded Theresa.

"No Theresa nothing is wrong, but how do you know that God loves me? I know that may sound like a silly question, but I'd like to know that you're not just saying that to make me feel good," Gabriel asked in a very serious but calm tone.

"Gabriel," Theresa was somewhat taken aback by Gabriel's comment, "what makes you say that, that's a hurtful thing to say."

"I'm sorry Theresa, I didn't mean it the way I said it," offered an apologetic Gabriel. "I'm just saying that I pray to God too, and God doesn't speak to me to tell me He loves me or anything, so I just assume God does love me. I don't have the certainty that you seem to have and I wanted to find out how your certainty came about," asked Gabriel.

"Gabriel, I know that God has heard my prayers because He manifests His response in actions or occurrences that then happen. I prayed He would help you find your way when you left the monastery and then you became a Monsignor to Cardinal Roncalli. That's how I believe God heard my prayers and what happened was His way of speaking to me. But, then again you were also praying that God would help you to find out what you were to do with your life and now comes this opportunity with Cardinal Roncalli. Was that not in reality an answer to your prayers? We were taught that when the multitude pray to God in a singular purpose that the combined voices of those offering up prayer to God has the magnified strength of getting God's attention, so to speak. He responds by actions not words. God always answers my prayers, but it isn't always to grant me my wishes. I believe that God speaks to us in many ways, and sometimes when He does, we may not always be listening. His answer is right there before us, but we may have turned a deaf ear, as the way the answer comes to us is one we reject. Nevertheless, it was right there before us."

"I know we need to be taking your statement on the Milwaukee inci-dent, but let me ask my question in a more direct manner. Theresa, do you hear the voice of God when you pray and feel that the voice is speaking directly to you?"

"Now I know why you asked me to be honest with you and since you asked, I will tell you. But I ask that my answer stays between the two of us and not Monsignor O'Grady, not Cardinal Roncalli, nor Mother Superior, and not even our Holy Father. Actually, not anyone while I am alive is to know. Please promise me that, Gabriel?"

Hearing Gabriel's agreement, Theresa responded, "When I'm praying I get so involved in my communication with God, I blot out everything else and I'm literally deaf to the world around me. Some of my fellow nuns have said that on occasion, when they've been asked to interrupt me in prayer by Mother Superior, they say that they have to yell at me or even shake me before they get my attention. I am that immersed in praying. They tell me that I'm silent in my prayers but that there is a glow of light that surrounds me that seems to be extinguished as I come out of my trance. In my head I can hear a voice saying, 'Yes, my child and bless you my child,' and sometimes during my confessions I even hear the words, 'You are forgiven my child.' It's not like having a conversation where I'm asking questions and getting a reply."

"You must think I'm nuts Gabriel, but I swear I do hear a voice and I believe it's the voice of our Lord or our Holy Father in Heaven. Once, one of the nuns told me that she saw me floating above the pew in prayer with a glow of light around me. I told her she was hallucinating and seeing things, as I've never had the feeling of floating nor have I ever seen any light that she or others have spoken of." Alarmed that Gabriel had fixed his gaze on her in a riveted manner with a stare so transfixed in an expression of disbelief, it frightened Theresa, causing her to blurt out his name. "Gabriel say something, please Gabriel say something, anything, you believe me don't you, please believe me, or am I crazy, say something!"

Slowly, Gabriel shook his head and was attempting to quickly gather his thoughts as to how to respond to Theresa, when Theresa jumped up from her chair and in a tearful voice replied to the silence, "That's it, I'm sorry I told you. I knew I shouldn't have said anything, that's why I've never told anyone. But I thought you might understand, but I can tell from the look on your face, you condemn me as would everyone else if they knew. Now, if you're done with me, I'm going to my room."

Finally, Gabriel in a stern tone that he did not mean to convey said, "Theresa, please sit down, Theresa sit down please. I believe you, I really do believe you and no one condemns you, nor should you believe anyone would. I think it's wonderful, please come return to your chair. You say that this nun saw you and described what was happening when you were in prayer. During these investigations, when conducted by Monsignor O'Grady, I am sure this will come up in your interview with him."

Slowly, Theresa retreated to her chair and sat with her head bowed and her hands folded in her lap in total subjugation. After she was seated, Gabriel did not hesitate in attempting to break the silence, but Theresa looked up and said in a tearful voice, "I am worried Gabriel, that in this investigation, things about me are going to be said, and I don't know what to do or how to reply."

"Theresa, you're saying that when you're praying and in communication with our Lord, you do not sense any change about your person or of your immediate surroundings. This is very important, because if you are asked anything about the light that surrounds you or your levitation, you can answer simply, 'I am not aware of any such occurrence,' and that will be the truth. Remember as your attorney, I will be there when you are asked questions and if I feel that those questions are inappropriate, I will be there to help you get through it. If you're too upset to go on, we can take your statement tomorrow."

Theresa shook her head and finally uttered a guttural sound, "No I'm fine, just give me a minute. I'd like to give my statement now if you're ready. I'm just embarrassed. It appears many nuns may have already come forward with what they observed, and I am now concerned with what they must think of me."

"No, those that have seen you believe you walk in the grace of God. They believe that you have been blessed in some way, and when they are near you, they feel closer to God as well as they feel His presence in you. That is why I wanted to speak with you before you spoke with Monsignor O'Grady."

"Will you be present when Monsignor O'Grady interviews me and takes my statement?"

"No Theresa, as he is co-counsel and his interview will be on behalf of the church. However, if the subject of what Sister Mary Gertrude or what others may have said to him is mentioned, simply say you have no awareness that you were doing anything other than praying. If he asks you if anyone ever told you about what they saw, simply share the nuns' conversations they have had with you and acknowledge that no one else has spoken of this to you. The main thrust of his investigation will be the incident in Milwaukee. If anyone other than Monsignor O'Grady raises any questions about the light or levitation, simply say, 'I can't answer any questions regarding such matters without the presence of my attorney, Monsignor Bonaci.' Do not volunteer to anyone to give any suppositions as to what you believe caused the vision. Just tell anyone that asks, the truth of what happened, what you saw, and what you heard, and that includes Monsignor O'Grady."

"Gabriel, this whole thing is preposterous. I don't know what happened in Milwaukee, but it wasn't because of me, I can assure you of that. I've never done anything to put myself in the position of drawing attention to myself. I don't want it or welcome it. I wish this whole situation hadn't happened."

"You know Theresa, I imagine that more than two thousand years ago, Our Blessed Mother was reacting in the same way when the archangel visited her, and told her that she would conceive the Son of God. You must find the strength in you as she found, to trust in God and let God do with you as He wishes."

"Gabriel, please don't compare me to Mary, I'm not worthy to be thought of in the same breath as our Lord's Blessed Mother. I know I will do whatever God wishes of me, but not what some humans determine as to what they believe should be wished upon me. Now, let's get on with my statement," Theresa concluded.

"Theresa, I know you will seek God's help in determining what He wants of you and I know you will do what is right in the sight of God. Let's begin the interview."

———◇———

Later that night, Theresa knelt before the crucifix in her small room to pray, choosing her room over the small chapel to afford her the privacy she felt she had never needed in the past. Current circumstances now made Theresa leery of those around her when she prayed. She was sure that she'd never be able to enter the chapel for private prayer with the same fervor that was now second nature to her in prayer. In the privacy of her room, with nothing but the crucifix and her rosary that she held firmly in her grasp, Theresa began her prayers.

"Dearest Lord Jesus, please hear my prayers as I kneel before You. I am frightened Lord, and I am so in need of Your grace and guidance. I am truly in an hour of need for You to show me what You want of me. I am so unworthy, and I am confused about what is happening and what happened in Milwaukee. I ask nothing for myself, but only to know what You wish me to do, and I will be obedient to Your wishes. I fear I have drawn attention to myself and I hope it is not true that I sought You to protect me during what happened in Milwaukee. Lord, I beg you to remove this attention that has come to me as there are millions more worthy than I that need Your protection. The children Lord, all over the world that are helpless, starving, homeless, and who are ill and dying need Your protection more than I. They face graver danger than I faced in Milwaukee. Send Your angels to protect them as they are being tortured and murdered by those that are evil and corrupt."

"Lord, I'm not sure how to ask this, but it is said that when I pray a glow of light surrounds me and they say that on occasion I levitate. These things bring attention to me that is unwanted. I seek only to be in Your grace and love, and seek nothing that would cast me in a light other than as Your unworthy servant. Please Lord, restore me to my humble place as Your bride who loves You and only seeks to be loved by You. If you wish Lord, I will endure whatever I must during these investigations. I will do so gladly in obedience to You and I will offer up all the duress on my part as penance for something I may have done in Milwaukee. Thank You, Lord, for hearing my prayers. Also Lord, I know You have heard the prayers of those in a tiny village in Somalia that has been attacked by rebel factions. The villagers are being held hostage in their little church with their parish priest. I ask that no harm come to them and that they remain safe, especially for the sake of the children and the priest who serves You. Good night Lord."

Chapter Six

In another part of the world in the jungles of a tiny country in Africa, rebel warlords fight for domination over an improvised land. Rival gangs strike fear in the hearts of the people of a tiny village that has too little to eat as they huddle in shacks barely standing. They seek only peace away from the bombs and gunfire heard in the distance. The tiny congregation, made up of mostly women and children, attempts to maintain a simple life where most of their males have previously been slain, captured, or forced to join another group of rebels set on the same path of terror and destruction.

At the break of dawn, convoys of thugs riding in old pick-up trucks, converted to armored vehicles, descend on the village on mud-filled roads that are little more than grooved paths in the jungle. They seek out the enemy, but more often, they seek out food, supplies, weapons and clothing. Unfortunately all too often, it is female companionship that is theirs for the taking regardless of their age or marital status. The victims are helpless against these hordes of mercenaries armed with AK-47's and other heavy military weaponry. Many of the victims have been converted to Christianity by the missionaries, such as the one that is now their village priest. Year after year, the wars rage on with apparent little concern from the modern world. Thousands die or are wounded as village after village suffers the steady diet of genocide that would not be tolerated in other parts of the world.

The United Nations peace keeping forces have long given up on their frustrating efforts to end the slaughter and bring humanitarian aid that often falls into the wrong hands and is sold for more weapons. Entire population shifts on the continent occur and more and more seek to escape the never-ending carnage. Each day is another day of brutal survival knowing no one cares as they are the forsaken, whose only reward will come in heaven. In the dark crevices of this African continent, little of the twenty-first century technology exists unless it can be found housed in the butt of an automatic weapon. If not from the slow death of starvation, illness or disease, death is swift from a wielding machete as the blood of innocents fertilizes the soil as the streams, puddles, and ponds run red with their blood.

Millions sit comfortably in their homes in Europe, America, Australia, and many parts of Asia who on occasion read with disinterest or frustration of the reports of these mindless killings. The old adage, 'there but for the grace of God go I,' is a source of little comfort or support to the millions being slaughtered each year. Yes, Gabriel Bonaci, former Marine Corps Captain who became Monsignor Bonaci had been one of those that helped evacuate civilians and missionaries during some of the bloody battles among the warring factions. It is moments such as this, that it becomes apparent that man serves other masters such as greed, corruption, and apathy. These villagers are little more than pawns in the trade-offs of a political, economic, and social world that is moving too fast to care for the least fortunate of God's children. Gabriel heard on the news that a village in Somalia was taken under siege by the forces of a new general. The general had seized power less than a month ago in a bloody coup that brought back vivid memories of Gabriel's previous tours of duty in the war-torn areas of the Middle East as well as Africa.

After Gabriel had concluded his interview with Theresa, he was deeply concerned as to what Theresa might encounter with Monsignor O'Grady in his interview with her and gave serious thought to sitting in on the interview. He had hoped to visit with Monsignor O'Grady to learn how his interview with Sister Mary Magdalena had gone, as well as his interviews with other nuns within the convent. But, unfortunately by the time Monsignor O'Grady had concluded his interviews, Gabriel learned that Monsignor O'Grady was on the phone with Cardinal Roncalli.

"Yes, Cardinal Roncalli is expecting your call," responded the Cardinal's secretary. "Your Eminence, Monsignor O'Grady is on line one."

"Hello Bob, how are you," the jovial Cardinal greeted the Monsignor. "I hope all is going well with your investigation, and I was looking forward to your call before speaking with Gabriel." One of the enduring qualities of the Cardinal was to establish a close relationship with members of his staff by using their first name when in private conversations to create a more relaxed atmosphere than the formal religious titles afforded them.

"Your Eminence," replied Monsignor O'Grady, who refused to use the Cardinal's first name when on the phone, especially in light of the serious matter he was about to share with the Cardinal. "It appears that we have uncovered a situation I had not anticipated and yet it may be the answer to our prayers." He then proceeded to share what he had discovered as related to Sister Mary Theresa regarding the glow of light surrounding her as reported by several nuns and a priest, as well as the sight of her levitation as reported by two nuns. "Isn't Sister Mary Theresa's real brother Monsignor Bonaci, and I'm concerned that their relationship may compromise our investigation."

"No Bob, as a matter of fact, if what has been said about Sister Mary Theresa is true, and obviously those expressing what they saw have no reason to lie, then Sister Mary Theresa is about to become the focal point of the biggest religious event since Fatima, Lourdes, or Guadalupe. She is going to need all the help she can get to weather this investigation. We are in a modern era of mass unlimited and instantaneous access to information transmitted around the globe by anyone with a cell phone, iPad, iPod, or computer. We must be prepared for a media blitz like we've never seen before."

"Then, you obviously agree with my conclusions regarding this heavenly event. We must determine if what was witnessed in Milwaukee was a visitation, intercession, or intervention."

"I agree with you Bob, we must find out, if for some reason and somehow, this event is intrinsically tied to Sister Mary Theresa. We must find out if that connection was just a visitation in which she was an innocent bystander, or whether she invoked the heavenly host to come to her aid. We also must know whether the heavenly vision was an intervention by

God of God's choosing. Bob, you must be diligent in your investigation and document every possible connection to Sister Mary Theresa and this event. We must also protect her from both the forces of evil and from those who, in their religious zeal, wish to cast her as some religious fanatic. Therefore, Monsignor Bonaci's presence will keep some from going overboard in this entire matter as he seeks to protect his sister. I will be in touch with Monsignor Bonaci to ensure he understands his role and understands your mission as well, and I expect complete and total cooperation between the two of you. Do you understand me, Bob?"

"Yes your Eminence, I do understand and will do as you've asked," promised Monsignor O'Grady.

As soon as Cardinal Roncalli ended his call, he dialed Monsignor Bonaci, and before the phone rang a second time, Gabriel, seeing a phone picture of the Cardinal on his cell phone, answered the call. "Hello your Eminence," answered Gabriel.

"Hello Gabriel, how are you, and have you had the opportunity to interview both Sister Mary Magdalena and Sister Mary Theresa? How are they doing and I hope you've conveyed my best wishes to them both and my blessings to them as well. It is very important for them to have your complete trust so they are willing to place themselves in your protective care as their attorney."

As was always the case, Cardinal Roncalli wasted no time or minced words in getting out what he wanted to say and ensure it was understood. He left no doubt in anyone's mind that he was in control and at the top of his game, especially when it came to matters of church business. He set a tone that you too better be at the top of your game, as conversations with him were strenuous mental exercises, and his verbal combative exchanges tested whether you had the stomach to go toe-to-toe with him. The faint or light-hearted were soon swept away by the mastery of his intelligence, wit, and verbal skill.

"Yes Father, I've met with both of them and each shared the same story or their versions of what we first understood had occurred in the exchange between them and the young men in Milwaukee."

"How are they holding up and do they appreciate the magnitude of what possibly occurred as well as their involvement in the whole situation?" inquired the Cardinal.

"Yes, Father, I detailed all that was involved, and they both are very brave, candid, and forthcoming in the experience they shared. Of course, they are both puzzled by the sighting."

"Are they now," the Cardinal said in a sarcastic but inquisitive tone that gave Gabriel a note of concern. He knew the Cardinal was never inclined to idle chatter or unwarranted speculation. "Gabriel, I've spoken with Monsignor O'Grady and he has shared some interesting insight into these two nuns, especially the one to whom you are related. Should I have any concern that your relationship to Sister Mary Theresa might prejudice a fair and impartial investigation into this entire matter?"

"Since my role is to provide legal counsel to them and ensure them of their rights both secular and ecclesiastical, I see no conflict or inability for me to perform my duties to the highest standards you've always required and expected of me, Father."

"Gabriel, Gabriel, let's knock off the BS, and you know better than to play games with me over what I need to know. If you're going to do a cover-up, protection act, or be an obstructionist to my getting to the truth and substance of this entire matter, then my considerable confidence in you has been sorely misplaced. Now tell me Gabriel, what have you learned about Sister Mary Theresa that you will want to voluntarily share with me," Cardinal Roncalli asked in a stern voice.

"Father, I gather that Monsignor O'Grady has shared information of the observations that others have made regarding Sister Mary Theresa. I cannot confirm nor deny at this time whether these observations are aberrations of their minds or real concrete revelations. I always assume Father you want the truth supported by facts and not hearsay or wild accusations. Sister Mary Theresa does not know by her own experience of the light that surrounds her in prayer, nor does she have the experience and knowledge that she has on occasion levitated as seen by others and shared with her. She does not know why the vision appeared and what caused it to come at that moment. All of what I am sharing with you will be detailed in my written report, including that Theresa did use the words, 'the Hand of God will protect us.' She claims she did not use the words 'I call on the Hand of God to protect us.' I believe the answer as to whether Theresa caused an intercession, asked God to intercede on her behalf, or if God, upon seeing her plight intervened on her behalf, is not an answer that I can provide. This is an ecclesiastical question that is best left to you, the Holy See, and Monsignor O'Grady."

"You see Gabriel, the matter of Sister Mary Theresa and the vision are not separate issues from the facts or observations made by others. The facts detailing the observations regarding Sister Mary Theresa must be borne out that she is, what she appears to be….." Before Cardinal Roncalli could go further he was interrupted by Gabriel.

"But Father," Gabriel interjected in a protective tone, "exactly what is it to you that she appears to be? I'd really like to know the answer to that," Gabriel spat out the words.

"Gabriel," Cardinal Roncalli spoke in a softened and compassionate voice, "Sister Mary Theresa may be one of those rare humans who walks in the grace of God and is blessed by His presence within her soul. We must at all costs and with all our efforts, protect her from those that might seek to exploit her goodness. She may be blessed, beatific, and may be saintly, but we cannot allow the intrusion of the secular world to harm her in any way. I believe she is the conduit to what occurred in Milwaukee and within her are the answers we seek."

"Thank you for your understanding and for your kindness and support."

"Gabriel, I love you as if you were my own son and I know I demand much from you. But, you cannot fail us in finding out whether we have just a truly good person or a saint living amongst us in Sister Mary Theresa. We must find out if there is a connection or just a coincidence between this child of God and the intercession or intervention that occurred. We must learn what we can expect from this connection, if it exists, as to whether it is a signal from God as to His coming now, or His coming in the near future. Will you do this for me?"

"Yes Father," Gabriel humbly replied then added, "but what of Monsignor O'Grady?"

"You leave him to me and if you find that in any way he is jeopardizing the investigation and not protecting Sister Mary Theresa or the Church, you come to me directly. Speak of this conversation to no one, now go in peace my son and God bless you and Sister Mary Theresa."

"Good night Father," Gabriel replied before ending their call.

The arrival of several armed vehicles and a transport truck with a dozen uniformed soldiers surrounded the makeshift church in the center of the tiny village in Somalia. The soldiers quickly exited the vehicles and set up a semicircle in front of the church, while another vehicle with a 50 caliber machine gun drove to the rear of the church and positioned itself at the rear door. Minutes earlier, the singing of hymns had been heard coming from the church as the congregation raised their voices in song and prayer. Now the singing fell silent upon hearing the roar of the engines and the clamoring of the troops as their leader shouted out commands to the soldiers to take their positions. Suddenly, the main front doors of the church were pushed in by the heavy boot of the rebel commander as all in the congregation turned to see the commander enter with two armed uniformed soldiers on either side of him. The priest, who had been conducting services, walked up the aisle toward the commander. As he walked, he held his hands together in an act of prayer and blessing, and spoke loudly so all of the congregation could hear his words. "Welcome to the house of the Lord, come join us in prayer for the salvation of our souls."

The commander spoke equally loud wanting the congregation to hear his reply. "Father, we are not here for salvation but we are here for those souls who provided safe haven to the rebels and we understand you are one of them."

The priest stopped as he came within a few feet of the commander and looked the commander directly in the eye and replied, "I have many in my flock that I attend to and I do not ask them for their political persuasions or beliefs. I only serve their needs to feed, shelter, and comfort them if they are ill or wounded."

"Oh Father," the commander said in a loud voice again addressing the congregation, you are a good man and a good servant to your people and I know your people love their shepherd as he loves his flock. But, I say to all of you, give me the rebels I seek, and place them before me and I will spare this man who is your priest."

Immediately, the congregation broke out in angered voices led by a woman who could be heard above all the others, "He is a man of God, please do not hurt him!"

The officer quickly grabbed a young girl who was sitting at the end of a pew and withdrew his pistol and with his left arm around the ten-year-old girl, put the pistol to her head. "It is of no consequence to me whether I shoot your beloved priest or this child. I want information on when the rebels were here, how many of them were here, and where did they go. Also, are any of them here now and who aided them while they were here. For each of these five questions on which I do not receive the correct answer, I will kill one member of your congregation starting with this young girl, then your priest, and then each of you as well."

The priest put his hand in the air as if in a gesture of offering a blessing and looked directly at the officer and said in a voice all could hear, "My people know nothing of what you ask. It was I and I alone that tended to the rebels in giving them shelter for the night and fresh clothing and food. They were here in the dead of night while all here were asleep and they left with my blessings before anyone in the congregation awoke. Do what you wish with me but leave my people alone."

"Ah Father, you are too good to be true how you protect your flock like the good shepherd. For me to shoot you and send you to heaven would be a reward. Well Father, you are not worthy of a reward for your punishment, nor will I make you a martyr for your people for they would have you sainted before the day is over. No Father, I will not shoot you. For your punishment, my men will tie you up and have you stand outside your church to watch it burn to the ground with all of your people inside."

Quickly, the officer threw the young girl to the ground and yelled to his men, "Take the priest outside and lock and barricade the doors with everyone else inside."

The priest's hands were tied behind his back and he was led outside while the congregation watched in horror. "Anyone that attempts to escape will be shot," the officer shouted and turning to the priest, said in a stern uncompromising voice, "Your punishment will be to watch your entire congregation go up in flames."

"No, no please do not do that," begged the priest. "Punish me not them, they are innocent."

The officer's men moved quickly to pour gasoline around the base and on the outside walls of the wooden church and brought additional tree limbs and brush to sustain the fire as the doors were blocked and the men posted themselves about the windows. Then the officer shouted, "Light the fire."

The priest fell to his knees and began to pray as Molotov cocktails were thrown through several windows. Soon screaming and yelling could be heard from within the church as the flames rose higher and engulfed the entire church as the branches, twigs, and brush fueled the flames. The officer and his men watched with little emotion or expression on their frozen faces as the dancing flames grew in intensity.

Suddenly, the clear bright morning became dark and claps of thunder roared across the sky and torrents of water poured down with a flooding rain that quickly extinguished the flames. The front and rear doors of the church suddenly burst open, exploding them off their hinges and pushing away the tree limbs that blocked the exits as a funnel of water swept through the church's interior and doused all the flames in a matter of seconds. High winds picked up to an almost gale force as the officer and the soldiers sought shelter among the vehicles from the driving and pounding rain. Then, the vehicles were struck by lightning bolts descending directly downward upon the vehicles. They exploded and burst into flames and continued to burn unabated by the pouring rain.

Out of the church came forth the entire congregation as the officer yelled to his men to shoot them. As the soldiers raise their weapons, the AK-47's and the 50 caliber machine guns exploded into pieces. The officer and the soldiers were in shock and confusion by what was happening and stood frozen not knowing what to do next. As quickly as the rain had come, the rain stopped and the winds quieted and the darkened sky grew brighter. Then, a flash of light appeared in the sky and there, towering over them, a huge angelic figure appeared and pointed his sword toward the soldiers as a booming voice from the heavens was heard by all.

"These are my people and my angels will protect them, now go and tell your leaders that the Hand of God will destroy any and all who seek to harm others that seek peace." The officer and his men quickly ran to the priest and untied him and the priest said to them, "You have seen the power of the Lord, now go in peace and may God forgive each of you." The soldiers gathered what they could and ran out of the village, far different men than had arrived.

Word of what happened in the village in Somalia was quickly picked up by the wire services, internet, and other media outlets as the word was spread throughout the world of another angelic appearance. But, this time the vision was accompanied by a heavenly voice. The media quickly picked up on the similarity of the two events, especially the words 'The Hand of God'. As word reached Cardinal Roncalli, he immediately called Monsignor Gabriel Bonaci on his cell phone in the middle of the night. "Gabriel, I've been on the phone with the Archbishop in Africa regarding a new heavenly vision in Somalia. Gabriel awoke instantly upon hearing of another heavenly vision. Cardinal Roncalli related the entire story that had been relayed to him.

Gabriel listened intently, and immediately and without any encouragement, offered the Cardinal an answer to a question the Cardinal had yet to ask. "Father, I do not believe that Sister Mary Theresa is aware of any situation in Africa. This has to be a separate incident totally unrelated to what happened in Milwaukee. The only way there could be a connection to Sister Theresa is that she heard about the incident on the late evening news when the story first broke and asked God in her prayers to intercede on behalf of the beleaguered priest and his congregation."

Pleased with the insight Gabriel had just shared, Roncalli said in an enthusiastic voice, "You never cease to amaze me that at times when I don't think any of my teachings have sunk into that cranium of yours, you show me moments of brilliance."

"Yes Father, I will immediately contact Theresa to see if her prayers included any intercession request concerning the incident in Africa. I'll also try to pinpoint the time she prayed versus the time the angelic vision occurred in Africa and reconcile the time difference. But Father, I do have one question and I'm not sure if there is an answer or if it is premature to ask. Since the Bishop in Africa called, I'm assuming that the church in Africa is a Catholic Church? We now have two incidents that are tied to the Catholic religion. I'm wondering if there is some significance that both have happened with those in our religion?"

There was a long pause before Cardinal Roncalli replied, "I have long believed that the Catholic Church was and is the first and true church of Christ. However, our history as an organized religion has been one checkered with incidents of heresy, deception, manipulation, and most certainly corruption, and falsehoods. That aside, I believe that today we've remained true to the tenants upon which Christ built His church. Why these visitations, intercessions, or interventions have been and continue with a connection to the Catholic Church should not be viewed or taken as through the Catholic Church has favor with God over other religions."

"As a matter of fact, we are not God's chosen people as told to us in the Old and portions of the New Testament. I do not buy into the theory that the Jewish faith's rejection of Christ was a direct cause of the suffering and pain that they have endured all these many centuries. I also believe that our enlightened ecumenicalism recognizes that other religions that are Christian are based on the belief that Jesus Christ is the Way, the Truth, and the Light. He that believes in Him and takes Him into their heart, mind and soul as their personal savior will be saved. In short, as to why the other religions that share our belief in Christ have not had a connection with these heavenly visions is a question for which I have no answer."

Luckily, Gabriel was staying at the convent as he and Monsignor O'Grady had a morning meeting to discuss their recent findings and clarify any differences between the testimonies each nun had given separately. Gabriel went to the Mother Superior's office and told her that Cardinal Roncalli had given him instructions that he immediately see Sister Mary Theresa. Certain questions needed to be asked of her, and she needed to answer them as Cardinal Roncali was awaiting her immediate reply. Within ten minutes, Sister Mary Theresa was knocking on the office door and as she entered she was surprised to see Gabriel.

"Monsignor Bonaci." Though surprised, she had the presence to address him by his formal title.

"Please Sister, I have just spoken to the Cardinal and he has requested that you be asked some confidential questions and he is awaiting an immediate reply. Mother Superior, with your permission, may we please have some privacy? We won't be but a moment."

Without a word, Mother Superior let herself out of the office and closed the door securely. As soon as the door closed, Gabriel turned to Theresa and asked, "Are you aware of an incident that occurred in Somalia in Africa last night?"

"Yes Gabriel, just before retiring, a brief mention of it was on the news, reporting that a rebel group had invaded a small village and was holding the priest and his congregation hostage. They indicated that later in the broadcast they would have more details. But I was too tired to stay up and I decided to go to sleep so I could meet with you and Monsignor O'Grady early this morning. I didn't expect that you wanted to meet with me this early before morning services, but Sister Mary Magdalena woke me to tell me you wanted to see me in Mother Superior's office."

"I take it that before you retired you said your prayers. Do you recall about what time you said your prayers last night?"

"Gabriel, what's going on, surely you didn't summon me here merely to ask me if I said my prayers."

"Theresa, I only need an answer to that one question and then I'll tell you everything. If you can, I need to know the exact moment to the hour and minute that you said your prayers."

"Gabriel, you've got to be kidding, really what's this all about?"

"No Theresa, I'm not joking and I am very serious and I'm not asking as your brother, I'm asking as Monsignor Bonaci. Now please tell me the precise time you concluded your prayers."

"It was about ten-thirty, I remember looking at the clock and realized how exhausted I was and not looking forward to rising at five in the morning for services."

"Thank you Theresa. Now, I need you to clarify for me a few more things, and then I will explain everything that is going on. In your prayers, did you ask for God to protect the priest and his congregation in Somalia from harm, and other than the brief broadcast on the news about the incident in Somalia, what did you learn before you retired?"

"Gabriel, well of course I did, why would you ask such a silly question.

Each night I always include in my prayers the need to ask God to protect you, Daniel, as well as mother and father and others. Why, have you learned more about what happened in Somalia, please tell me?"

Gabriel walked over to the T.V. in the office and turned on the news station where the event of the incident in Somalia was being broadcasted. The foreign correspondent related the entire incident of the rebel leader's intent of burning the church down with the entire congregation inside for aiding those fighting the rebels. The news continued as to how an angel appeared and saved the priest and the congregation as the fire that was engulfing the church was put out by torrents of rain and wind. Gabriel reached out to turn off the T.V. when Theresa stopped him. "No Gabriel, please leave it on. I want to hear more of what happened from the foreign correspondent's interview with the priest and members of the congregation."

The priest related to the correspondent what he and the villagers had experienced when the angel appeared above the village with a flaming sword and saved all of them. He told how the angel destroyed the rebels' equipment, as the rebels fled into the nearby jungle. Gabriel allowed the T.V. to remain on for several more minutes and then without hesitation turned it off to gain Theresa's full attention.

Now looking straight into her eyes, Gabriel knelt before her and said, "Theresa, I must concur with what the Cardinal and Monsignor O'Grady have said. You are the conduit that is bringing this angel to intercede and causing the events in Milwaukee and now in Somalia in response to your prayers."

"No Gabriel, I do not understand, you can't possibly believe that I'm involved in this incident in Somalia. This has to be some kind of coincidence. In no way am I involved!"

Theresa fell to her knees holding her hands over her ears as she began to sob, "No Gabriel it's not me, I'm nobody. God just did this as He helped me in Milwaukee, and now He has helped the priest and his congregation. God responded to my prayers for help and He has responded to the priest and his congregation's prayers for help. God is the conduit not me, you've got to believe me Gabriel, please."

"You haven't heard the whole story, the priest and members of his congregation said that they heard the voice of God admonishing the rebels saying, 'You have now seen the Hand of God'. Do those words ring a bell and sound familiar to what you yourself said in Milwaukee?" said Gabriel, his voice rising in frustration.

Suddenly, there was a pounding on the office door and Mother Superior yelled out, "Is everything all right, may I come in, please open this door."

Gabriel went to the door and opened it and Mother Superior quickly stepped in and closed the door after her. "Now Monsignor Bonaci, I have been most cooperative and understanding and even supportive of the work you've been asked to undertake at the behest of Cardinal Roncalli. But, I will not allow you or anyone else to come into my convent and brow-beat my nuns and create a continuing disturbance in my home and sanctuary. I suggest you return later in the morning and we can discuss this matter further as your business here has ended. Have I made myself clear to you in this matter as I will be happy to discuss your intrusion with the Cardinal if that is what you wish me to do?"

Gabriel nodded, "I am very sorry and I apologize that I've upset you." But before Gabriel could continue, the Mother Superior interrupted him with, "No Monsignor, you have not upset me, you have angered me. It will require that I now do many hours of penance for this anger to be forgiven, so if you will leave, Sister Mary Theresa can return to her services."

Chapter Seven

Sister Mary Magdalena entered the confessional to seek the protection afforded by the act of confession in the sacrament of penance in the Roman Catholic Church, as the only place she could secure the privacy and confidentiality she needed. Here, she sought help to alleviate the anguish and torment of her every wakening moment over these past several weeks.

"Bless me father for I have sinned, and I am in need of God's help for I have had thoughts of a man that are inappropriate, harmful, and could lead to the temptations of sin if not sin in of itself."

The priest, acting as the servant of God replied, "Please child tell me how old are you?"

"Father, it is not a matter of age, for I am an adult of twenty-seven years. But, I am a nun and a bride of Christ. A man has come into my life and he is the kind of man that I never believed I would find in my lifetime, and he is a priest. I have never had these feelings for a man until I met him. He knows nothing of my feelings for him, but now my thoughts are of nothing but him."

"Does this man have feelings for you and has he said anything to you to encourage the growth of your feelings for him?"

"No Father, I do not know if he has feelings for me, as he has conducted himself in the highest standards of moral, ethical, and professional conduct. Nor, have I indicated to him that I am having these thoughts of him in the manner that I have shared here in the confessional. Each time that I am with him and learn more of him, my feelings grow stronger and my thoughts of him have caused me to betray my vocation and betray our Lord as well. This has now given rise to my thoughts of leaving my vocation entirely."

"My child, you do not want to be the cause of creating doubts within him about his vocation and you should pray to the Holy Spirit to strengthen you against the forces of evil and for the Holy Spirit to enter you mind, heart, body, and soul to help you ward off these temptations of sin. It is best my child that whatever the circumstances are that bring you together, you must make every effort to avoid contact, as innocent as it may be, for the salvation and sanctification of both of your souls. Can you do that my child?"

"The circumstances that have caused us to be together are unusual and are not in my control for the foreseeable future, as I'm obligated to work closely with him. But, I will do what you have mentioned and ask for God's forgiveness so my soul may be healed."

"Please seek the help of our Blessed Mother as she may guide you to accept the will of God and what God wants for the salvation of your immortal soul. Please say the rosary ten times as your penance. Now go in peace with the forgiveness and blessing of God."

Once Gabriel was in his room he called Cardinal Roncalli on his direct line and was surprised to hear a jovial voice as the Cardinal was amused by his recent encounter with the Mother Superior. "I have just hung up from Mother Superior's call and while she understands you are only doing your job, she warned me that if I continue to disrupt the sanctity of her convent that she has the authority to kick both you and Monsignor O'Grady out, on what she terms as 'your blessed rears'. So tell me Gabriel, what information do you have for me as I've been on the phone with the papal secretary in Rome and he wants answers as to what is causing these heavenly visions."

Gabriel quickly and without any melodrama responded, "I have confirmed that the timely prayer of Sister Mary Theresa did coincide with the adjusted time between Holy Hill, Wisconsin and Somalia in Africa. Therefore, she could very well be the conduit through which the heavenly angel was interceding on her behalf in response to her prayers. Now the big question before the Church is how to proceed with this belief to both the religious and secular community to acknowledge that among them is one who walks with the grace of God. Another question is how do we protect her and find out what God's plan is for this saintly nun who communicates with God."

"Gabriel, I believe you have been called to a higher purpose than as my executive secretary. You have a responsibility to ensure that your sister and the entire Bonaci family is protected from those who would want to exploit this child of God, as well as those in this world who would want to gain power over her for their own gain."

"Surely Father," Gabriel offered, "God will protect her as we've seen."

"Gabriel, the ways of men and the ways of evil are beyond our human ability to control the forces that will be unleashed if Theresa were ever to fall into the wrong hands. She must be protected at all costs and that responsibility will fall on you. She will be held in high regard in the Church and there are those that will want to start the process of beatification while she is alive. Others will want to attribute miracles to her and ask that she prays for God to intercede on their behalf and so much more. How Sister Mary Theresa responds will be watched with great interest. It may not be what she wants while she is alive and she may wish that none of it had ever happened. She needs guidance and support and to be surrounded by people she trusts and those that will love and cherish her. She must remain grounded by the counsel of those around her and must remain a cloistered nun for her own protection."

"But Father," Gabriel interjected, "Sister Mary Theresa does not believe all that occurred in Milwaukee and Somalia are of her doing, and she does not want to be treated in any special way and only wishes to remain unknown but not as a cloistered nun. She wants no part of this and seeks to deny the things that are said about her as having the ability to summon heavenly hosts. She believes that she is not worthy to be thought of in any context other than as a servant of God and bride of Christ."

"Gabriel, her wish to remain unknown may not be possible for the world is clamoring for an answer as to why suddenly a heavenly host has appeared twice in the space of a few weeks. She appears to be our only answer as to why this is happening. Now please Gabriel, do as I ask and surround her with those that will protect and guide her in the coming days and weeks."

Sister Mary Magdalena sat quietly in the Mother Superior's office awaiting the arrival of Monsignor Bonaci. She no longer wears the habit of her order, having now been granted permission to join the order of Sister Mary Theresa, and has chosen to wear the modern garb of those at Holy Hill Convent where Sister Mary Theresa resides. Her long ankle-length skirt, with a high-necked long sleeve blouse over which she wears a long bolero jacket creates a garment that allows the nuns to blend in with the secular community they serve. Another major difference is that her hair is allowed to be free of any cover as it loosely frames her face revealing auburn tresses that give hint to her Welch ancestry. Since her last confession, she continues to struggle with her growing attraction to Monsignor Bonaci, and she is extremely nervous in now meeting with him. She assumes the purpose of the meeting is to be asked more questions as to his investigation of the incident in Milwaukee.

The door opens slowly and she is surprised to see the Mother Superior enter, but then she notices that Monsignor Bonaci is following closely behind, as they both come to stand in front of her as she rises to greet them. It is the Mother Superior that begins the conversation. "Sister Mary Magdalena, as you are new to our order, it is not our custom that you be allowed to visit alone with a man even though he is your attorney and a Monsignor of the church. However, since on prior occasions while here under our care, you have met with him during the investigation of the incident in Milwaukee, I will permit it, but only if you are in agreement."

"Yes Mother Superior, for the purpose of continuing the investigation I agree to visit with Monsignor Bonaci." During the exchange between the Mother Superior and Magdalena, Gabriel was surprised by the change in appearance of Sister Magdalena in her new garb. He now saw her as a young woman, rather than as a black-habited nun. As Magdalena spoke,

Gabriel's eyes were riveted upon her, and feelings began to awaken within him that he had not had in a long time.

"Well then, I will be in the library if I am needed and you can reach me there when you've completed your meeting," concluded Mother Superior. Both Gabriel and Sister Mary Magdalena waited to speak until the door was completely closed ensuring the Mother Superior had departed from earshot.

With her usual confidence, Magdalena opened their visit with an enthusiastic greeting, "It's good to see you, Monsignor Bonaci."

"Why so formal Sister Mary Magdalena, we are alone and Father Bonaci or just Father would be better, especially in the light of my coming here to ask a great favor of you. One day I would hope that as we become friends, you would be able to call me Gabriel when we are alone."

"I see," smiled Magdalena, "Gabriel is a rather nice name, and I too would be pleased if you were to address me as Maggie when we are alone."

"Is Maggie your real name or is it a nickname for Magdalena?" asked Gabriel.

"No, actually my real name is Margaret. I grew up as Maggie O'Dowd but I took the name Magdalena when I joined the convent and took my vows. As you know, we all take Mary as our first name in the same way as when boys are confirmed, they take the name of Joseph as a second or third middle name."

"Good then, that will make it so much easier to discuss the reason for my visit with you."

"Father, I mean Gabriel, why were you staring at me when Mother Superior and I were conversing, have I done something wrong?"

"Wrong, no not at all, you have done nothing wrong and I apologize if you thought I was staring. I was adjusting to your transformation from the black garb of a nun to seeing you in your new outfit that is similar to the one worn by my sister Theresa. Am I to understand that you have now joined the Sisters of Charity here, at Holy Hill, Wisconsin? Actually, your new garb suits you better as it is more in line with how I envisioned you as a person based on your background that I reviewed as a part of the investigation regarding the incident in Milwaukee. For some reason, learning about you and your past does not lead one to think your path would be to become a nun."

"So you've investigated me, have you now, and you don't think of me as being the kind of a person who would choose to become a nun?"

"I'm sorry Maggie, I didn't mean anything disparaging by my observation, but with you having graduated college, gone to law school and having had a secular career, you entered the convent at an older age than most. Your background is not the usual path that most girls take in selecting a religious vocation. Plus, with your outgoing manner, your ease at verbal exchange and your air of confidence, these too are not typical of a person that becomes a nun. Actually, you remind me so much of Theresa."

"So, I remind you of Theresa, except without her pious demeanor and godly attributes. Well Gabriel, let me share with you that I too find it hard to believe based on your background that you would choose to become a monk."

"How may I ask, did you learn of my having been a monk?" Gabriel asked.

"Well, before being a monk you were the big man on campus, lettered in four sports, and you were an All-American in football, plus a Marine Corps lawyer, and later a war hero. That is not exactly the background that would lead one to believe you would become a cloistered monk."

"Well, you have me there, but how do you know so much about my background?"

"I mentioned that your sister and I have become good friends and when I asked about you, she opened up like a gushing spring. She is so proud of you and loves you so much, she can't stop talking about her big brother and personal hero. Yes, I believe Theresa and I are very much alike except that she walks in the grace of God and has truly embraced her role as the bride of Christ. I believe sometimes that I became a nun for all the wrong reasons based on my background. Yes, I do have a different background than what most nuns possess. I got to see the world and all its negativity. I had horrific experiences as a child with poor role models for parents who did not paint a pretty picture of marriage and parenthood. The men I met in college and at law school were not sterling candidates for marriage. I also saw much evil in the world as to the greed and corruption of mankind. I chose not to deal with any of it and escaped to the convent, probably in the same way as you seemed to have done in becoming a monk."

"Maggie, you are so insightful and correct that I saw evil in the world, especially on the battlefield. Therefore, I sought God's help on an exclusive basis to better understand why God allowed evil to persist and allowed it to overcome good. But, I learned that the monastery was not a place for me, and I hope in my new role, I can continue to serve God. Frankly, these revelations in Milwaukee and Somalia are strengthening my belief that God is active in the world and is willing to take on evil to allow good to win in the end. I'm sorry for pontificating, but I believe that you and I are very much alike and that makes it so much easier to ask this great favor of you and I sincerely hope you agree."

"Yes, Gabriel, as I shared with you earlier, Theresa has made a great impression on me and we have become good friends. I want her to be more in my life as I believe it will be good for me as well as my soul. Please tell me what it is that you want and need me to do as I know in my heart, I will agree to it."

"I must ask that whether you agree or do not agree, this request is strictly between us, even to the exclusivity of Theresa. Based on the investigations that Monsignor O'Grady and I have conducted, and with the counsel of Cardinal Roncalli, we believe Sister Theresa is the conduit through which these visions of the angels are taking place. We believe that Theresa asked God to intercede on behalf of both of you to protect you from being harassed by the youths that confronted you. We also believe that Theresa asked God to intercede on behalf of the priest and his congregation in Somalia. We do not know why God has chosen to come forth nor do we know why He is answering Theresa's prayers to intercede. We don't know if more intercessions will occur, but we have seen two in less than a few weeks. As the world, both religious and secular, are demanding explanations as to the visions in Milwaukee and Somalia, Sister Mary Theresa may become the focal point of public scrutiny. We know that she will not be able to continue her current role, especially administering in the community among the poor and homeless, without placing herself in serious jeopardy. She is going to need care and protection by those she trusts and those that love her. She will need someone to run interference for her as the world learns of her direct involvement, and they will seek her out for her to intercede on their behalf. The Church, Cardinal Roncalli, and her family including myself, will do what we can. But, we cannot be with her twenty-four hours a day nor can we ask the secular institutions to give her twenty-four hour protection as well."

"No," interjected Maggie, "but I can be the one that she can trust. She knows that I love her and will protect her. She will know that I will be there for her when she has the need to share her plight with someone. Gabriel, I want to be that person. You have given me a purpose in my vocation and a purpose that will allow me to fulfill my vows. But, more importantly Gabriel, I will be given the opportunity to be able to care for a person who walks in the grace of God."

"Our first task is to meet with the Mother Superior to ensure she is involved in our plans. We do not want to alter current convent life so Theresa would be viewed as being favored over the other nuns. Precautions must be taken to ensure security is increased on the grounds and around the convent walls so Theresa may move about without fear of intruders or the media photographers wanting a picture of her for their tabloids. We also want to be sure that Mother Superior will acquiesce to allowing you a room near Theresa, and that your activities within the community of sisters melds with those of Theresa. We must be sure that the other sisters do not feel that Theresa or you are receiving preferential treatment. Theresa will not be allowed to work outside the convent to serve the nearby community as she now does. While you will be permitted to travel as you currently do, your travel may be restricted if it is discovered that you are the one that has special access to Theresa so as to place your safety in jeopardy as well. Now tell me honestly Maggie, after what I've shared with you, do you still want to undertake these tasks?"

"Yes Gabriel, I say it in all honesty and sincerity. I pledge to be a companion, friend and true sister to Theresa."

"Thank you Maggie, Theresa is and has always been headstrong. I believe you are as well, and for that reason, the two of you will make a great match in strength of will and purpose. I hope for all our sakes you both are kept safe. I would like you to be with me when we meet with her to help share this new reality that must now be her life from this day forward. Now, we must first meet with Mother Superior unless you have some questions or even some objections."

"The only question I have Gabriel, is how am I to stay in touch with you to communicate information that you may want to know on how Theresa is doing, or if she needs help that I may not be able to provide? How often will you be coming to the convent and how will I know in advance of your coming?"

"Good question Maggie, Theresa may not have visitors other than her family and any such visitors are going to need approval from me before they may be scheduled to meet with her. So you will act as Theresa's secretary to determine such scheduling and I will give you my personal phone number so you can reach me day or night. Sometimes you may be required to meet with Cardinal Roncalli, Monsignor O'Grady, or myself at the church office in Chicago to act as a liaison for Theresa in her duties and tasks here at the convent. Remember, we must ensure that Mother Superior never feels that she is not in charge of her own convent nor should others be challenged to feel that they are being excluded in any way. I know this is a tremendous responsibility you've undertaken, but I feel you are the only person who can do this. If for any reason you feel that I have asked too much of you, I do not want you to hesitate in contacting me immediately, and I expect you to be candid and forthcoming as to your concerns."

"Gabriel, you have my solemn promise that I will always be open and honest with you in any matter that comes between us as a part of my vow of obedience and service to our Lord."

Maggie reached out with both hands to grasp Gabriel's hands and held them tightly as she was about to leave. "Gabriel, thank you sincerely, you will never know how appreciative I am for the confidence and faith you've placed in me and I won't fail you."

With their hands still grasped together Gabriel acknowledged her departure, "Go in peace and may God bless you for all you are about to do." Maggie quickly turned to leave, and as they released their hands, both felt a charge of electricity and emotion that went through the both of them.

The meeting with Mother Superior lasted less than an hour. Gabriel was more than pleased how the Mother Superior had responded to his various requests. She was extremely supportive and accommodating to all the arrangements he had enumerated. It was obvious she clearly understood what needed to be done. Her positive response was proof of her love for Theresa, and she was confident that Sister Mary Magdalena would be a great asset in assisting her in the many necessary changes the convent would undergo.

However, Gabriel's elation soon ended within minutes after Theresa and Maggie joined them in the Mother Superior's office. "So, what you're saying," Theresa loudly challenged, "is that I am to be a prisoner here in the convent and not be allowed to perform my duties among the poor, homeless and starving people in our nearby communities? Nor, will I be allowed to care for them on behalf of our Lord. Why are you doing this, you above all others Monsignor Bonaci, have betrayed me. All because you and others believe that I'm the cause of these visions in Milwaukee and Somalia. Now you want me to live as a cloistered nun locked away from the world. Well Monsignor Bonaci, I'm not going to do it for you, Cardinal Roncalli, or even our Holy Father in Rome. When I took my vows, it was to be a servant of our Lord doing his work here on Earth as long as there was a breath of life in my body. I won't let my vocation be one of solely praying in silent piety, thinking only of my own soul's redemption and salvation."

It would take more than an hour to get Sister Mary Theresa into a frame of mind to agree, at least on a temporary basis, to some changes until the clamor of the angelic visions had died down. With no video recordings of the angelic vision in Somalia, it was felt that the clamor of the media following the incident in Milwaukee would soon be abated if no other visions appeared. It took all three of them with various forms of compromise, reasoning, cajoling and pleading to gain her support to undertake what they wanted her to do. No doubt, Theresa had become extremely upset and distressed by what she believed would be the end of her life as she had envisioned her vocation to be.

"All right," Theresa said with finality, "I will do what you ask but only until the media circus that has been created dies down and I can return to a normal life here at the convent. But, I warn you, especially you Monsignor Bonaci, I won't stand for any more of this gibberish that I am anything more than the lowest of the low as a servant of the Lord. I won't have anyone putting me on some pedestal as deserving any more attention than any one of our other nuns who serve the Lord daily with little notice or reward. Have I made myself clear to all of you? Now, I must go to chapel and ask for forgiveness as to how I've spoken to you and regain the ability to be an obedient servant to our Lord."

The three of them looked upon in amazement for they had never encountered what could be termed as the wrath of God descending on them from one that had never uttered a word of anger and frustration. As Theresa stopped and turned to leave the office, she said to Gabriel, "May I please have your blessing Monsignor Bonaci, though I am not worthy of one?"

"Yes Sister Mary Theresa Bonaci," Gabriel said as he distinctly enunciated each syllable of her full name, "may God bless you and go in peace."

After Theresa had left the office, Gabriel turned to Mother Superior and Sister Mary Magdalena, "I know that was not easy. Thank you both, I must now report to Cardinal Roncalli on what we've done for the good of our Church, and especially for Sister Mary Theresa."

Chapter Eight

Less than a week later, the best laid plans of mice and men would be severely disrupted. The evening news again brought what was happening around the world into living rooms with the speed of technology as the evening was unfolding.

"This is Rosalie Garcia of MKWZ in El Paso, Texas reporting on an update of an incident in the small town of Esperanza, Mexico. Across the border near El Paso, a dozen members of one of Mexico's largest drug cartels has taken over a school, holding one hundred children hostage. They demand that the local authorities acquiesce to their demands that fellow gang members, including the gang's leader, be released from the local prison in exchange for the safe release of the children. The wire services and news media outlets are on the scene and have generated national and international attention as to the plight of these children. The Mexican Army, in support of the local authorities, surrounded the school in a standoff that is now going into its second day as night falls. Authorities indicate that the cartel refuses to release even the youngest children. The authorities are threatening to shoot the leader of the cartel if any of the children are harmed. We have a live feed from Marta Lopez reporting from the scene on the school grounds."

"Yes Rosalie, the school grounds have turned into an armed encampment and we've learned that the children are being held in the windowless gymnasium in the center of the school building. The regional governor of the Chiwarra Providence is expected to be here to speak personally with the captors. Hundreds of parents and family members of the children maintain a vigil behind the barricades fearing the worst for their children's safety. The imprisoned leader of the cartel, Arturo Fuentes, has sent a message to the captors that he wants the children released unharmed. It appears that world-wide public opinion has turned against them to end the standoff. This is Marta Lopez reporting from Esperanza, Mexico as we wait to learn more on how this crisis will end."

"Thank you Marta, you've now heard of the efforts to free the children. We have been informed that though the children are frightened, they are being treated well by their captors as computers within the school have been set up by the captors with Skype capabilities to allow the children to speak with their parents. We are told that the vending machines within the school have been emptied of food and drink and that otherwise the children are being well cared for. This is Rosalie Garcia continuing our coverage of the hostage situation in Esperanza, Mexico."

Meanwhile, in a private chapel on the convent grounds in Holy Hill, Wisconsin, Sister Mary Theresa is concerned for the hostage children in Mexico. She asks in a plea to God to protect and free the children unharmed and release them into the welcoming arms of their parents.

"Dearest Father, please intercede on behalf of the children in the name of your blessed and beloved Mother of all children, our Blessed Virgin Mother Mary, to free them unharmed from their captors. I ask this in the name of your Son, our Lord Jesus, and I will do whatever penance or suffering you ask for the sake of the children's safe release."

Within minutes of Sister Mary Theresa's prayer, in the night sky of Esperanza, Mexico, there appeared over the school a glow of light that grew brighter with each passing moment until the light became almost blinding in intensity to those standing vigil. The light descended downward engulfing the school and from the brilliance of the light, dazzling sparkles of flashes came alive and the glow of an image of an archangel came into view. Emanating from his sword, flashes of light were directed toward the school. An awe of amazement and surprise arose from all present as they all knelt and made the sign of the cross. Then, as quickly as the vision appeared, the light was extinguished as if a candle had been blown out, and the sky was plunged into darkness once more.

Within seconds, one of the doors of the school burst open as the children began pouring out and then a second door opened and more children poured out. The police and army personnel from their various positions began to enter the building in rapid succession as the barricades were pushed aside and could no longer hold back the throng of parents rushing to reach their children. Within minutes, all of the children had left the building and were quickly accounted for amidst the chaos and confusion of children and parents embracing. The various news media outlets sought to interject themselves into the melee with microphones being thrust into the faces of the older children. The police and army personnel were dragging out the captors that seemed semi-unconscious and totally submissive. As soon as the captors were observed, the media ran to where the police had set up a perimeter within the barricades to protect the crime scene and establish order.

Some of the older children were allowed by their parents to speak to the media as to how they were able to escape from the captors. One of the youths said that the gym was plunged into darkness for a second and then sparkles of twirling lights danced about the gym as they saw each of the captors collapse and fall to the floor. In conversations with the police, the media was able to learn that they found the captors unconscious in an almost semi-comatose state but they were alive and breathing on their own. They were hauled off to prison and all the weapons that they had were confiscated.

However, the real story that was foremost in everyone's mind, now that the children were safe and their captors were in custody, was whether all present had seen the vision of the angel and the light display. The media that had been recording the event was attempting to determine whether or not any of it had been captured and recorded. The news media was in a frenzy interviewing people as to what they saw and heard. Each of the people that were asked by the media wanted to render their own version as well as their opinion. Did they see the light? Did they see the globes of light circling the school? Did they see the flashes of light and did they see the vision of an angel emerge from the light? Lastly, did they see the sparkles of twirling light emanating from the angel's sword? Yes, each observer over and over again shared the same affirmative response as to what they saw and all were of the opinion that they had seen a miracle. Confirming that the brilliant light had been able to be captured by the cameras there at the scene, including the vision of an angel, the media spread the vision across all its outlets and channels throughout the world. Instantly, millions upon millions were provided the vision on their cell phones.

Also within minutes, Cardinal Roncalli, upon seeing these images on his television and listening to the testimonials of those present at the scene, called Monsignor Bonaci. "Gabriel," Roncalli bellowed into the phone, but even before he was able to identify and confirm it was Gabriel, he received a loud response.

"Yes Father, I was expecting your call."

"I'll bet you were, so what do you make of this latest incident in Mexico. This is the third incident within three weeks of each other and it is going to ramp up the demands for an explanation. It appears this particular event didn't involve a nun or a priest. But with the Mexican people being primarily a Catholic nation, I believe the Church will still need to come up with an answer as to what is going on in the world. Again, here's what I need you to do, and I know you may disagree with me almost to the point of disobeying me, but you must do what I ask."

"Father, I may disagree with you and have done so on occasion, but I have always done what you ask and never would I disobey you," Gabriel retorted in a serious tone. "I know what you want Father, and since I'm staying at the convent, I will get Mother Superior to allow me to visit with Sister Mary Theresa to ask if she in any way prayed for God's intercession in this incident."

"You know me well Gabriel, and you have learned well. I ask you to forgive me for doubting you, but yes, please get me that answer immediately and call me back."

After receiving Mother Superior's approval to see Theresa, Gabriel also asked if he could first meet with Sister Mary Magdalena before having Theresa join them. The Mother Superior, fully aware of the incident

THE INTERCESSION OF GOD 91

in Mexico, easily granted Gabriel's request. As soon as Sister Mary Magdalena entered Gabriel's office and the door was closed, Gabriel realized the intimacy of the situation. Even though Maggie had been awakened from her sleep, Gabriel still found himself deeply attracted to her and grateful he was able to be with her. However, he maintained his usual friendly but business-like pretext, hoping she had not picked up on his attraction to her. "Maggie, I'm sorry for not thinking how I'm putting you in an uncomfortable position in meeting me alone before seeing Theresa. But, I need your help in ensuring that Theresa doesn't feel uncomfortable like she did following our last visit, and where she feels she is again being accused of something that she has done wrong."

"Gabriel, you are a very good and kind person, and I know you love Theresa. I have seen you watch over her to ensure that in these situations, you have always had her best interest at heart. I would not have agreed to your requests to help you if I felt in any way that Theresa's well-being was not always foremost in your mind. I am aware of the incident in Mexico and I knew you would be calling. I'm here for the both of you if I can be of help."

"Thank you Maggie, Cardinal Roncalli requested that I immediately speak with Theresa to see if she prayed for God's intercession in this latest incident."

"Yes, I was with Theresa last night before we retired after evening services and we were able to catch the evening news reporting the incident in Mexico. Knowing Theresa, I bet that she thought nothing of it to include in her evening prayers, a request to our Lord to protect the children. This evening she said she was going to thank God for protecting the children, so I know she knows everything that has transpired in Mexico. I only recommend Gabriel, that awakening her at this late hour, you should be as gentle as possible with her and not be as accusatory as you were regarding the incident in Somalia."

"Yes Maggie, you're right. I'm going to deal with this in a far better way than before and I'm glad you're here to help me do that."

A knock on the door somewhat startled the both of them as they heard Theresa's voice call out Gabriel's name, asking if she could enter. She was surprised as she entered to see Magdalena alone in the office with

Gabriel, and she was not sure of what to make of Sister Magdalena's presence. "Gabriel, you asked to see me at this late hour, is something wrong? Sister Mary Magdalena, I wasn't expecting to see you as well with Father Bonaci, surely something must be very wrong."

"No," Gabriel tried to reassure her, and realized that Maggie's presence alone with him in his office was awkward for Theresa to understand. He tried to make some effort to ease his embarrassment that he knew was shared by Sister Mary Magdalena as well.

"I'm sorry for the need to awaken the both of you at this late hour, but Cardinal Roncalli wanted me to ensure that you were aware of the incident in Mexico. I told him that I was confident you were and yet he wanted me to confirm that situation with you directly."

"Gabriel, I'm sorry Cardinal Roncalli saw the need to lessen your sleep as well as Sister Mary Magdalena's, when I would have been more than happy to confirm in the early morning that yes, I was fully aware of the entire situation. Also Gabriel, I know you'll want to know that the prior evening I did ask that the Lord intercede on behalf of the children. Seeing the news this evening and confirming they were all right, I thanked our Lord for His help. Now, is there anything more you need to know before Sister Mary Magdalena and I are able to return to our rooms?"

Gabriel was surprised by Theresa's candid admissions and her rather casual and dismissive attitude regarding the magnitude of what had occurred. "You did hear the report that there was another angelic vision involved where the whole world was able to see and confirm what happened?"

"Yes Gabriel, I did see the angelic vision and if you and Cardinal Roncalli want to attribute that to my prayer to intercede on behalf of the children, then so be it. I'll accept that blame together with the other two as well, if that is what you wish. Now, if you'll allow Sister Magdalena and me to return to our rooms, we bid you goodnight." Turning to Maggie, she said, "I'm sorry that Father Bonaci felt you had to be involved in this evening's conversation."

Sister Mary Magdalena gave Gabriel a puzzled look as though she could not think of any more to say as she moved toward the door to leave before hearing Theresa say to Gabriel, "I believe you owe Sister Mary Magdalena an apology."

It was then that Maggie found her voice and strength to say, "No, no apology is necessary, I have pledged to the both of you that I will do what I can to help you, Father Bonaci, and the Church through these investigations of these angelic sightings."

"Thank you Sister Mary Magdalena for all your help, and I do apologize for awakening you this evening and promise to be more considerate in the future," meekly replied Gabriel.

As both nuns left Gabriel's office, Theresa confronted Sister Mary Magdalena. "I know it is none of my business and I do not want to pry into the lives of others, but Gabriel is my true brother and you are my best friend and I love you both. But, being close to the both you, I have noticed glances and an exchange of looks that indicate there has come about a change in the relationship between you and Gabriel. I see it in his eyes as well as yours when you look at each other and how both your voices change in tone when you speak to one another. Please Maggie, tell me I'm imaging things, or what is going on between the two of you?"

"Oh Theresa, I'm so afraid to tell you how I feel and burden you with more things to concern you on top of all that is going on with these angelic visions. But, I have feelings for Gabriel and I believe I am falling in love with him. I don't know how to handle these feelings because of our situation as a nun and priest."

"I take it, that you and he have conversed about the situation. What does he say as to how he feels, as it's apparent his feelings toward you are similar to your feelings for him?"

"No Theresa, that's just it. I have not said anything to him about how I feel, and he has said nothing to me about how he feels. I only know that I'm fearful as to what his answer will be and I don't want to upset him as we are still both bound by our vocational vows. I'm so confused, I don't know what to do and I don't want to hurt him in any way. He's your brother and no one understands him better than you do. What should I do Theresa, please help me."

"I know him well enough to know that the way he is acting around you is not typical of him as a man. I have seen many women literally throw themselves at him. His response to them, while always considerate, is that he never gives them any encouragement. That was true when he was in college and throughout his military career. Obviously, since he entered the monastery and took his vows, I have never seen him show any interest in women in any romantic way. However, and I don't mean this as an encouragement to you, but since I've seen you two together, I've see him acting differently with you than any other woman he has met. I can only tell you that whatever is going on is not a good situation for you both. I believe that the both of you need to reconcile what is happening for the sake of your vows and for the good of your souls. Because I love you both, you both need to seek within your mind and your heart, what it is that each of you truly want as well as what the Lord expects of each of you. Now, go to Gabriel and tell him how you feel and give him a chance to respond so the both of you can move forward with your lives and do it in the grace of God."

As they both embraced, each parted to their respective rooms, both with the heavy burden that their lives were at a crossroads and both needed the help of the Lord to guide them to the correct path. Now in her room with the glow of a candle, Theresa knelt before the crucifix that hung above her bed and she began her prayers. "Dearest Jesus, please hear my prayer. I do not know what is happening and I need your guidance so I may do Your will. I am frightened by some of the things that have occurred and more frightened by Gabriel's words that I am the cause of what is happening. Please give me the wisdom and understanding of what You want me to do and fill me with the Holy Spirit to have the courage and strength to act in a way that reflects my love and my commitment to You."

Suddenly, the glow of the candle grew brighter and brighter until it totally illuminated the entire room. A still brighter light cast a strong ray of light on the crucifix, and suddenly sparkles of lights appeared around the crucifix. Theresa's eyes were fixed on the crucifix and she was filled with the Holy Spirit, as a calm and comforting voice spoke to her.

"Do not fear My child, I am with you today and for all the days of your life and I will be with you forever when you come to dwell in the house of My Father."

Immediately, Theresa closed her eyes and bent her head and body in supplication to the presence of God and she quietly whispered, "My Lord and My God."

Again the voice spoke to her, "I have heard your prayers Sister Mary Theresa and those of your brother Gabriel, and it is now the time for My return to put an end to evil and to bring peace on Earth. What you have seen is that My angels will come before Me as evil will be swept away and I will come to judge those that still have evil in their hearts. I will take unto My bosom those that have believed in Me and the Earth will prevail in peace for one thousand years as forty generations will have been cleansed from their sins and made ready for the final judgment of mankind."

The light in the room dimmed and the candle flickered one last time and went out as the room was plunged into darkness and Theresa remained immobile on the floor clutching her rosary as she fell asleep. The next morning in chapel as the nuns assembled as they did each morning at five-thirty, all were present except one. Mother Superior, as was her custom, did a headcount and discovered Sister Mary Theresa's absence. She requested that Sister Mary Magdalena go see what was keeping Theresa from the morning services being conducted by Monsignor O'Grady with Monsignor Bonaci in attendance. Less than five minutes had passed when Sister Mary Magdalena came rushing into the chapel and went directly to Mother Superior and whispered in her ear. The Mother Superior abruptly stood and rushed to Monsignor Bonaci as the two then followed Sister Mary Magdalena from the chapel to Theresa's room.

Sister Mary Magdalena was the first to enter, pushing the door open as the other two followed her in. There on the floor lay Theresa sprawled face down with a glow of light surrounding her entire body. Without hesitation, the Mother Superior touched Theresa to feel for a pulse and to see if she was breathing. As the Mother Superior bent over Theresa, the glow of light surrounded them both as Gabriel and Maggie looked on with awe and concern and stared in amazement as the glow of light that enveloped them grew brighter.

"She's all right," declared the Mother Superior. "Quickly, Sister Magdalena, get me some cold compresses and Monsignor, get me a glass of water for her." The Mother Superior cradled Sister Theresa in her arms until the others returned. Within minutes, Theresa's eyes began to flutter open. She appeared dazed and not aware of her surroundings until she was able to focus on the Mother Superior's face hovering over her. She attempted to mouth some words, but nothing came out as she was offered some water to drink. "Now take this sip of water," Mother Superior offered as she dabbed Theresa's head with the cold compress. After a few sips of water, Theresa was able to say, "Thank you Mother Superior, what happened to me?" It was then she noticed Gabriel and Magdalena above her and her eyes brightened at the sight of them. "Come Monsignor," Mother Superior directed, "help me to get Theresa onto her bed so we can make her more comfortable."

Once Theresa was settled and some color had returned to her face and her breathing appeared normal, Mother Superior turned to Gabriel and Magdalena and said to the both of them, "I expect the both of you will say nothing of what you saw this morning. While I have the authority to order you, Sister Magdalena, to a vow of perpetual silence, I can only hope you too Monsignor, will honor my request." But before either could respond or allow the Mother Superior to utter another word, Theresa found her strength and her tongue to say loudly, "No, wait, you must listen to me."

"I remember saying my prayers to our Lord Jesus, and as I did the small candle there on my dresser became brighter and brighter as I continued to fix my eyes on the crucifix as a glow of light surrounded it. Then, as sparkles of lights danced around the crucifix, I heard a voice speak to me, and the voice that spoke to me was the voice of our Lord telling me to tell our Holy Father in Rome an important message for all of mankind."

"Tell me Theresa, did our Lord tell you that this message was only for the ears of our Holy Father?"

"No Mother Superior, our Lord said nothing like that. But, I would like to repeat what He said to the three of you while it is fresh in my mind so I will be able to remember it better when I speak to the Holy Father." Sister Mary Theresa was able then to recite word for word what Jesus had said to her. All three were captivated by every word she shared.

Forgetting any formality at the conclusion of what Theresa recited, Gabriel said in amazement, "Theresa, our Lord has shared His coming with you and has revealed His plans for all His people. With your permission, I must tell Cardinal Roncalli of what has happened as he will help ensure an audience with our Holy Father as quickly as possible."

"Yes Gabriel, I want you and Cardinal Roncalli to accompany me to

Rome and with Mother Superior's permission, I would like to have Sister Mary Magdalena accompany me as my traveling companion."

"How wise of you Sister Mary Theresa to know that you should have a nun as one of your traveling companions, even though one of them is your biological brother," the Mother Superior assured her.

"Well then it is settled, we'll begin the preparations immediately and be prepared to leave for the Vatican within the next few days if Cardinal Roncalli is able to ensure that our Holy Father will be there to greet us."

Chapter Nine

The following morning, knowing that Monsignor Bonaci had been asked by the Mother Superior to perform mass and hear the confessions of the nuns of the convent, Sister Mary Magdalena decided to take advantage of this opportunity. Within seconds of hearing the words, "Bless me Father for I have sinned," Gabriel knew that it was Sister Mary Magdalena on the other side of the confessional screen. His first instinct was to pretend that he did not know it was Magdalena giving her confession. Also, he hoped that she would not recognize him. But, Magdalena proceeded to let him know that no coincidence or mistake had occurred.

"Monsignor Bonaci, it is I, Sister Mary Magdalena, who has come to give you my confession and I believe I need the protection of the confessional. I believe my confession needs to be heard by you in the presence of God within the blessed sacrament of confession so you know I only speak the truth that abides in my heart and soul."

"Sister Mary Magdalena, you know that while in the sacrament of confession, I am not Father Bonaci nor Monsignor Bonaci but only a servant of God as God listens to your sins and transgressions. If you wish to speak to me in another manner, we need to adjourn to my office within the convent."

"No, I want the presence of God to witness what needs to be said of my sins and transgressions. While they are mine and mine alone, they need to be heard by you in the presence of God as part of my confession."

"I cannot turn you away from seeking confession, especially if you feel my presence will enable you to form a true confession before God. I will hear you as God hears you."

"Father, since my last confession of two weeks ago, I have sinned dozens and dozens of times and that has prevented me from receiving communion with our Lord. This is a sin in of itself. I have given a great deal of thought to the removal of what causes me to sin. But, I have come to believe these transgressions would not stop as they continue to magnify themselves with each passing day. I have thought of leaving the convent and forsaking the vows of my vocation. However, I realize that it would not remove my agony and heartache nor prevent these thoughts from invading my mind and heart."

Gabriel was extremely uncomfortable within the confines of the confessional as a priest administering the sacrament of confession with Magdalena. But, for her sake he chose to continue to listen in silence. Finally, Magdalena stopped and asked, "Father Bonaci, do you understand what I am trying to say?"

Gabriel replied in the strict context of the confessional, "No my child, I do not know what is troubling you. Please tell me specifically, what is the sin that is causing you to violate the laws of God and those of your vocation?"

"Father, I have met a man and I have come to know and love this man. I have thoughts of this man that are not in keeping with the vows of celibacy of my vocation. These thoughts pervade every moment of my waking being and I have dreams of him that are in conflict with my role as a bride of Christ. This is an abomination to God and our Lord. I never thought I would ever meet such a man and have such feelings of love for him that cause me to want to be with him every moment. I have never shared these feeling with him nor do I know whether those feeling would be reciprocated as he has never in any way shown or told me how he feels."

Gabriel knew that how he responded within the confessional must be as God would want him to respond or he would violate his role in the eyes of God. "Sister Mary Magdalena, what you have felt and what you are experiencing is not unique. Thousands within their religious vocations, if not millions, have had those feelings at some time or another. God intended us to love one another and God intended for a man and a woman to love one another. In that love, they come together in marriage in a bond to bring forth children as a family. God created those feelings within the very fiber of our beings and taking the vows of celibacy does not make those feelings go away. These are gifts from God allowing for men and women to love from the time of the first creation of Adam and Eve. Those feelings are in the natural order as to how God intended them to be. Our free will allows us to set aside our willingness to participate in what God has meant there to be between a man and a woman. But, the feelings we have are still there as part of the very fiber of our beings as created by God. Some religions, knowing the great and unnatural task of celibacy have permitted marriage between a man and a woman within their vows of becoming a member of their clergy. The ability to love, Sister Mary Magdalena, is an emotion of the highest order as it is the foundation and basis upon which God created mankind whose source stems directly from the divinity of God's love."

"Father, I know what love is, but I am not speaking of my love of God, or God's love of me, or the love between a parent and a child, nor of siblings, or our love of mankind. I'm speaking of my love as a woman for a man and his love for me. I'm not sure I can continue to set that love aside even for my vows."

"Magdalena, you know our Lord Jesus is divine and One in the trinity with God the Father, and the Holy Spirit, yet Christ was also a man born of a woman and as man had all the feelings of any man born as a human. Christ as a man had those feelings to love a woman, but He had to forsake those feelings for what He knew was expected of Him as the savior of mankind. His human love for Mary Magdalene and her love as a woman for Him had to be forsaken by the both of them. Christ also encouraged His disciples that they too needed to forsake the natural order of man and leave their wives and families to follow Him in their role of establishing His church on Earth."

Sister Mary Magdalena understood this of Christ, as well as the need of His followers, to forsake the love of another person for the love they had for Christ, the God. She also knew that she, through the vows of her vocation, was also a follower of Christ. But that was before she had ever met a man like Gabriel. While she did not want to forsake her love of God, she now believed she could not live without the love of this man. She did not intend to speak in a voice louder than her usual tone and volume in a confessional as she blurted out, "Gabriel, I am not a saint nor are you the Son of God. I love you as a woman loves a man, now do you love me in the same way before the eyes of God?"

Gabriel's mind was immediately filled with many thoughts and emotions in attempting to respond to the question that Magdalena had placed before him. Gabriel finally replied, "Sister Mary Magdalena, I believe you to be sorry for your sins, and for your penance you are to pray to God to help you determine your path in life. You are also required as your penance to confront this man and speak to him outside of the confessional to receive the answer to your question. Now go in peace, your sins are forgiven."

Gabriel, after giving the blessing, immediately stood and left the confessional and returned to his office in the convent.

There in his office he knelt and prayed. He knew the torment that raged in the heart and soul of Magdalena, for it was the same torment he had felt these past several weeks as he too had fallen in love with her. He knew that while he had said what needed to be said within the confines of the confessional as a priest, as a man he could barely contain himself in wanting to give her the reassurance of his love for her. He bowed his head and asked God to help him to know what God wanted him to do at this crossroads in his life. He then proceeded to call Cardinal Roncalli regarding God's visitation that had occurred earlier that morning with Sister Mary Theresa in her room while she was praying.

"Yes hello, this is Monsignor Bonaci, may I speak with his Eminence, yes thank you I'll wait." Within minutes, a familiar voice came on the line.

"Hello Gabriel, how are you this morning. The news is certainly abuzz with the incident in Mexico and everyone in the media is drawing comparisons to the incident in Somalia and Milwaukee and it is only going to get worse. The Holy Father and the Holy See are looking for some answers as the whole world has been turned upside down. Hopefully you have some good news for me so I can make some sense out of all of this."

"Father, I'm afraid that what I have to share will only give you more cause for concern and I'm sorry to have to share this with you over the phone."

"Gabriel," interrupted the Cardinal, "you know I hate prefaced conversation. Just spit it out, I'm a big boy if you haven't noticed, what's up?"

Gabriel shared what had happened and repeated word for word what had transpired with Sister Mary Theresa in the communication she had with the Lord. He also shared his idea as to the need to visit with the Holy Father as soon as possible. He outlined his plans to include himself, the Cardinal, Sister Mary Theresa, a chaperone for her in Sister Mary Magdalena, and possibly Monsignor O'Grady as well.

The Cardinal interjected, "Did she say that our Lord communicated to her that the Holy Father needed to be told directly what the Lord had shared with her?"

"No Father, Theresa felt that she needed the Holy Father to know what had been communicated to her. Other than Mother Superior, Sister Magdalena and I, no one else has knowledge of this visitation."

"Good, I believe that I must hear for myself, directly from Sister Mary Theresa, as to what she was told by our Lord before calling the Holy Father. I have questions that need to be asked and I would like to have the presence of Monsignor O'Grady there as well. When can you, Sister Theresa, Sister Magdalena, and Monsignor O'Grady come to Chicago to talk before we proceed to leave for Rome? Believe me, the Holy See will be a lion's den rivaling the Coliseum in Rome and our Holy Father may even be at a loss in controlling even those closest to him, once they know what Theresa has to share. The scrutiny and cross-examination of her will rival a court of law in which she will be presumed to be having hallucinations, be outright lying, and worse. She may be judged to be possessed by the devil before it is ever accepted that she walks in the grace of God. That is why we need the Holy Father to hold back the pack of wolves that will want to devour her. It will be a difficult time for her as well as for the rest of us and they will try to push Sister Mary Theresa to the brink of believing it was a dream, a fairy tale, or a figment of her imagination. Sister Magdalena, who was with Theresa when they both saw the angelic vision, will also come under their scrutiny. You, as their attorney will have your hands full providing evidence of the testimony from the boys in Milwaukee, and the thousands there that saw the vision. Testimony from the priest and congregation in Somalia needs to be gathered and lastly, the testimony from those who saw the vision in Mexico will need to be put forth into evidence. The pictures that were able to be taken by the media and others with cameras in Mexico and Milwaukee will be needed as evidence of these angelic visions."

Gabriel could only muster a quiet, "Yes Father, I fully understand what I must do."

"No Gabriel, I do not believe you do, your sister's health, life, and her very sanity may be placed in jeopardy until she is believed. Are you, and more so is she, prepared for such an ordeal. We have a serious obligation to ensure that she has been prepared for what will happen in Rome and even later as the world comes to know who she is."

"What do you want me to do?" asked Gabriel.

"We must ensure that Sister Mary Theresa is willing to accept that she does in fact have God's favor. She must believe that she walks in the grace of God and is held by God in the highest esteem of the Lord. Further, she must believe that she has been afforded the blessing of not only an intercession, as well as a visitation, and maybe even the intervention of God himself. We must get her to accept that in her prayers to God, she invoked the Hand of God to intercede not only for herself and Sister Mary Magdalena, but for the priest and his congregation, and the children in Mexico."

"But Father, Theresa will refute that she is anything but the lowliest of the low in the eyes of God and she does not consider herself to be worthy of God's favor, nor does she believe she should be held in God's highest esteem."

"Good, that is really a far better approach, but she must accept that her prayers to God may be what invoked the angelic visions to have occurred. We can better justify the connection of our Lord's visitation with Theresa in telling of His coming once we've established with the world that these visions were brought about by Theresa."

"Father, I know what I must do now," acknowledged Gabriel.

"Good," concluded Cardinal Roncalli. "I believe that your sister is a saint walking among us that has yet to be recognized and canonized. What do you think, Gabriel?"

"In a way, I have known that about Theresa all my life," Gabriel replied. "What does this all mean? Is this the fulfillment of Revelation that our Lord is truly coming to Earth to judge us and set apart those that have not believed in Him? Is this the 'make way for the coming of the Lord' moment?"

"As I've often said, my finite mind often finds it difficult to fully appreciate or even understand and comprehend the infinite mind of God. Often, I'm required to go on my full faith and belief in Him as my God. God has His own time frame for what He does or doesn't do and your guess is as good as mine as to what that may be."

"Yes Father, but millions of people around the world are turning to us for answers. Millions of people need to prepare themselves for His coming and they will turn to us for guidance. We will be found wanting for our failure to have not done our job in tending to our flock and the millions more that have lost their way that now need to hear the word of God."

"As the Lord has foretold, the Lord is coming but we know not when, as He may come in the dead of night while we are sleeping or as we go about our daily business. Nevertheless, we need to be ready and prepared for His coming whenever that may happen. Gabriel, please tell Sister Mary Theresa that I will invite your parents to join all of us for lunch in Chicago before we begin the arduous task of getting down to business in preparation for our visit to Rome. Good night Gabriel."

Much of the world was not privy to what was happening regarding the angelic visitations. In certain parts of the world, people lived in distrust and hatred as they were exposed to the propaganda of dictators and fanatical extremists. Whether they were atheists or agnostics who had filled their hearts with evil, these extremists were determined to destroy or enslave others that did not share in their beliefs. The Middle East had for many years become a hotbed of anti-Zionist and anti-American fervor. These religious radical zealots had set out to destroy those who opposed their way of life. They disregarded how contrary their beliefs were to fair and equal treatment of all humans, regardless of their race, gender, nationality, religious beliefs, customs, or origins.

The bright hope that was once promised by an Arab Spring had fallen to overwhelming forces of death and destruction at the hands of these radicals bent on world domination and genocide. Those that stood in their way or objected to their demonic beliefs became their enemy. Their bravado had been fueled by a prior indecisive U.S. President and his conflicting overtures of U.S. support to the Israeli nation which gave rise to a more confident Iran ready to make good on its promise to wipe America and Israel off the face of the earth.

Now, in the early morning hours, deep in the caverns hidden from view and camouflaged between two mountain peaks, six nuclear missiles stood ready to launch with their calibrations set and targeted for six locations in Israel. The devastation would be total and almost ten million souls would join the millions before them that perished in the Holocaust. A joint Syrian and Iranian army were poised to wipe out any fleeing Israelis that tried to escape the Armageddon that was about to ensue.

The ten-minute countdown had begun that armed the missiles as the Iranian scientists and military personnel began to clear the missile launch site. As the countdown reached less than the one-minute mark, suddenly the earth began to shake but the movement was not from the vibration of the rockets. The Iranian scientists saw on their instruments a seismic movement of untold magnitude that indicated an earthquake was taking place. They began to make every effort to shut down the launch, but the seismic register was now plowing past eight point zero and peaking higher. The ground below the missiles gave way and the rockets having achieved blast level began to sink and disappear beneath the earth. As the tips of the missiles disappeared below ground, the nuclear warheads exploded with the likes of which the world had never seen. The eruption of the warheads, together with the earthquake, caused the two mountain peaks to explode in all directions for miles, creating a huge crater as if a large meteor had stuck the Earth. The quake and explosions were felt for thousands of miles as aftershocks continued for several minutes at high seismic levels. The tremors and quakes were picked up by scientists around the world and satellite images were conveying the most horrifying spectacle known to mankind as clouds and plumes of nuclear gases were thrust thousands of miles into the atmosphere.

Suddenly from the rubble amid the nuclear dust, there appeared a bright light that easily challenged the brightness of the nuclear explosion that had happened moments ago. The light formed into the appearance of a golden angel that rose above the destruction. He appeared to be hundreds of feet tall and in his hand he held a flaming sword and extended the sword to the earth that had swallowed the missiles as a thunderous voice boomed out, "Behold the Hand of God!"

Soon, word reached the Syrian and Iranian armies positioned just beyond the borders of Israel to withdraw, but the word had come too late. The Israeli forces unleashed attacks of heavy air and ground missiles and wiped out both opposing armies. Within hours, after the fighting had ended, the presidents of Syria and Iran called for an emergency session of the United Nations. A joint resolution was presented before the entire body condemning the Syrian and Iranian nations and calling for the arrest and removal of the heads of both governments. Nations from all over the world called for them to be tried as war criminals as well as banning any of the leaders in those governments from attending the joint session. U.N. peace keeping forces were sent to quell any civil unrest and restore order in both of those countries. The United Nations established an interim governing body of nearby Middle Eastern nations including Israel to help establish free elections in Syria and Iran for their eventual self-determination under new constitutions.

In another part of the world, Cardinal Roncalli and the others had concluded the Bonaci family reunion luncheon and were now alone to discuss the preparations for their trip to Rome, when their meeting was interrupted by the Cardinal's secretary. "Your Eminence, please turn on your T.V. to see the televised report of the devastation from the war between Israel, Iran, and Syria. The reports are that all U.N. members are calling for a worldwide meeting of peace talks in New York. The U.N. wants to ensure that there will be no escalation by any nation against any other nation by enforcing a ceasefire among all nations. As the news was in progress, all turned to see photos and videos of the devastation of the nuclear holocaust as well as the photos of the angelic vision that hovered over the site. The news media attempted to piece together the set of circumstances that had preceded the confrontation and included in their reports the series of recent angelic visitations in Milwaukee, Somalia, and Mexico as well as the one at the site of the nuclear holocaust.

Monsignor O'Grady broke the stunned silence. "Well, I guess that ends our meeting with the Holy Father in Rome." Before he or the others could comment, the phone rang on the Cardinal's desk. The Cardinal answered the phone and listened for several minutes to what was being said as the expression on his face took on a somber look of deep concern as he concluded the call.

"No Monsignor, quite to the contrary, the meeting will go on but the location will be in New York at the United Nations. His Eminence and religious leaders of all faiths from all over the world have also been summoned to the peace talks in New York. It appears that the angelic vision at the nuclear site is being reported all over the world. The secular leaders are demanding answers from the religious community as to what is the meaning of all these visitations of angels that have recently occurred." Cardinal Roncalli then directed, "We need to get a chartered flight to New York where our Holy Father, together with several Cardinals, will meet with us two days before the U.N. meeting. The Holy Father wants to listen to what we have to report and he personally wants to meet with Sister Mary Theresa and our group."

"Monsignor Bonaci, please arrange for our flight and hotel accommodations in New York and we'll leave in the morning. We need to spend the rest of the day going over what we will say to the Holy Father and his staff when we meet with them. I believe that the world may need to be readied for our Lord's return and what better way than to unveil His announcement before all the world's governmental and religious leaders. Our teachings and scriptures have foretold many times that God's angels have preceded the heralding of those times when God has spoken to His people."

As all listened attentively to the Cardinal, it was Theresa who chose to fill the silence as the Cardinal concluded his comments. "Your Eminence, you speak of our teachings and what you believe, but I do not know why

I have been drawn into this situation. I am but a servant of our Lord and know nothing of God's plan for His people other than what He said to me in my prayers."

There was a pause, in which all the others present thought that Theresa would continue, but Cardinal Roncalli said without hesitation, "Sister Mary Theresa, actually you know better than all of us, for our Lord has spoken to you, and the world needs to hear what He has said. I believe that the Lord heard your prayers and those of the faithful, and that He has come to realize the plight of His people as He has so often in centuries past according to scriptures. Yes, in recent years we have not heard of any direct or overt response to our prayers as we have now. But, in the past, according to scripture, did He not hear the prayers of Noah and show His retribution to those that had defiled his creation? Did He not save those that were faithful to Him? Did He not hear the prayers of Moses to save His people from the scourge of the Pharaoh, and later did He not hear and respond to the prayers of David and the other prophets as well?"

Theresa immediately interjected with surprise and astonishment. "Please do not place me among those you speak of; I am no prophet, nor am I a leader of people. I am nothing but a bride of Christ who only seeks to be a worthy servant of our Lord. Please do not place me in the company of those that have been exalted by God. I am unworthy and humbled."

Suddenly it was Cardinal Roncalli who interrupted Theresa. "Did you not hear of our Blessed Mother's plea when the archangel came and announced that she was to become the Mother of God? She said, 'Why me, how can this be'. She too was a humbled servant of God, only a little older than a child herself, and yet she was accorded a high place among all of God's children. Who could have foreseen the choosing of Mary among all women on Earth? No Theresa, you are who you are because God wants that to be. You are the one that has been chosen by God to be an instrument of His salvation, and an unheralded witness to His return. Whatever you believe about yourself, believe that you walk in the favor of our Lord and He and only He needs to understand, appreciate, and determine why you, among all others in the world, have been chosen to tell of His coming."

It was Gabriel that then added, "Theresa, you have throughout your life placed your fate in the hands of our Lord as you continue to trust Him and continue to be His obedient and submissive servant bending your will to what He wants of you. Can you not continue to do as you have done, Sister Mary Theresa?"

Theresa's eyes filled with tears as they ran down her cheeks. She stared at those assembled before her, and as she looked up, she responded clearly, "I will do what the Lord asks and I place myself in His hands and will announce to the world in New York what He has asked me to share with them."

"Good," Cardinal Roncalli replied, "now let's get ourselves to New York and meet with our Holy Father."

Later that evening, Gabriel and Sister Mary Magdalena were alone in helping to arrange for their departure to New York. Though more than a week had passed since that day in the confessional, both seemed to pretend that it had never happened and the tension in the air that hung between them was very palpable. Though busy with the impact of the recent events, each had spent countless moments in thought as to how to proceed to bridge this void. Now that they were alone, it was Maggie that found the courage to ask, "Gabriel, have you given any thought to the question I asked in the confessional?"

"So often this past week I have thought of nothing else. I secretly acknowledged to myself shortly after we met that I felt there was something special going on between us. But, I frankly thought the feelings I was having were only on my part and I felt at a loss as to how to deal with them. As time passed, my feelings grew stronger and the torment I felt became more unbearable. As we came to know each other better, I was amazed that though I had never had those feeling for a woman before, I was having them for you. Yet here we are, a priest and a nun, both vowed to the lives of our separate vocations. At times, I felt that you may have feelings for me as our friendship grew and I so enjoyed our times together. But, I felt I had no right to burden you with my confusion to have you question your vocation. I frankly felt that I was better off not knowing how you felt about me. Then, you proceeded to present me with one of the biggest challenges in my entire life when you told me that you loved me.

I was not prepared, especially in the confessional, to hear your admission of your love for me, and I was confused about how to deal with it in the confessional."

"Oh Gabriel, I'm so sorry for doing that to you in the confessional. I was being cowardly to hide within the confessional and blurt out those feelings. But, all the torment you say you have been feeling these past several months that we've known each other, I was feeling that torment as well. Gabriel, while I am so happy to hear of your feelings for me, the question I asked in the confessional was, do you love me? We aren't in the confessional any longer, but I need a direct answer."

"Maggie, I do love you. I too have fallen in love with you more than you could ever know or understand. But, now that we both know the answer to our feelings for each other, it merely complicates the question as to what do we do about it. I am a priest and you are a nun, and both of us are pledged to our vocations and to the absence of a love between a man and a woman. Until that is resolved we can't move forward, no matter how much love exists between the two of us. This is a very difficult and challenging time for us both, and we can't let the love we've acknowledged interfere with our service to God, our vocation, and especially our commitment to Theresa, especially in light of our meeting with the Pope in New York."

"Gabriel, thank you for your courage in sharing the truth of your love for me; the enormity of that knowledge makes me want to run to you and embrace you. But, I too know of the impediment that exists before we can do more than acknowledge our love. I pledge that in the light of that love, we first focus on the task that God has asked each of us to do. Then, together with God's help we can find a way to the true fulfillment of our love for each other."

Without hesitation, Gabriel reached out his hands and extended them to Maggie. She grasped his hands and held them tightly as Gabriel said solemnly, "Yes Maggie, I agree that if our love is ever to be, we cannot forsake our love of God and what we must do to make way for His coming." A knock at the conference room door interrupted their conversation and the moment and the mood was lost.

The next evening as Maggie and Theresa settled into their hotel room less than a block from the United Nations building, Theresa commented as to how impressed she was with their plush accommodations. "You know Maggie, sometimes I feel that I've missed out on so much of the world that I haven't seen. I've never been to New York and I was so looking forward to going to Rome and seeing the Vatican. Entering the convent at such an early age, I never got a chance to travel. I guess you could say that I've lead a very sheltered life. While Chicago has its share of bright lights and tall buildings, New York seems to have so much more. I wish we could just explore some of the places near the hotel, but I know that Cardinal Roncalli and my brother have told us to stay in our room. The papal guard standing outside our door would not appreciate our trying to sneak out."

"Well, just listen to this little rebel in you, wanting to sneak out into the New York nightlife. I'm sorry to bust your bubble, but during some of my years in college and law school, some of my friends and I came to New York and all those lights and glitter hide the darker part of the city with its crime, filth, and the people that are really dangerous. There are people right outside this hotel that couldn't care less if you fell dead right in front of them, they'd just step over you and keep on walking."

"Yes, I'm sure you're right, even Chicago and Milwaukee have their dark sides as I've seen the homeless sleeping in the streets and in the alleys. I've seen some so hungry, they scavenge the garbage bins looking for food, and then huddle around a burning barrel for warmth. What bothers me the most is seeing some children barely clothed and sick also rummaging through the trash behind restaurants and stores for discarded food and warm clothes."

"Theresa, as I said, New York may have more lights and glitter, but it also has more of the darker side of life as do hundreds and hundreds of other cities across this country. When some of my friends returned from trips to Europe, Asia, South America, as well as Africa, they saw that we had in the United States, though small in comparison, the same squalor and deplorable conditions as those other countries."

"I guess I'm nervous about meeting the Pope tomorrow and restless because I know I won't get much sleep tonight. I'd really like to just step outside and get some fresh air and forget about what I'm going to confront before the religious leaders. Doing some people-watching on the sidewalk in front of the hotel and experiencing the lights, sounds, and smells of the city might do me a world of good. But, what's more important is to find out whether you and Gabriel have had a chance to talk about what is going on between the two of you, and whether each of you know what you're going to do about it. I have never seen Gabriel so pleased with himself, especially when he's in your presence."

"Theresa, after we spoke I did something that was absolutely terrible to Gabriel and you'd be shocked to know how cruel I was to him. First, I went to confession with a priest from one of the parishes near the convent and asked for God's forgiveness for the thoughts I was having about Gabriel that I felt were preventing me from taking communion."

"Maggie, you've got to be kidding! Did he know that you are a nun and that Gabriel is a priest? What did the priest say when you told him?"

"Yes, I know I told him that I was a nun, and whether or not I told him that the man I was speaking of was a priest, I really can't remember anymore. Anyway, he was very calm about it and told me to seek guidance from our Lord and then say a ton of Hail Mary's and ask for God's forgiveness. But it gave me the idea to pull the same thing on Gabriel. So a week later, when Gabriel was hearing confessions for the nuns at the convent, I went to him in the confessional."

"No Maggie," Theresa shouted, "I can't believe you really did that, knowing Gabriel as I do, you must have thrown him for a loop, so what happened?"

"Your brother's reaction was not what I expected. He became very serious and very professional in his demeanor, acting as if it wasn't him I was talking about, and he started telling me that the confessional was not the place to have this conversation."

Again, Theresa's excitement in learning what Maggie had done, caused her to blurt out, "Surely he knew that it was you on the other side of the curtain or did you let him know it was you that was speaking to him?"

"Oh yes, he knew it was me, I made sure of that, even using my name and his, so there could be no misunderstanding. Within seconds, he had recognized my voice and at first he wanted to end the confession and threatened to leave the confessional. He was in a state of denial while performing the sacrament of confession, insisting he was not Gabriel but God's emissary. He spoke of this man I was referring to as someone other than himself. He struggled with what was the right thing to do, whether to deny me confession, or hear my confession. But, he refused to speak to me as Gabriel, acting only as a priest would in hearing my confession. He went to great lengths to help me understand that while in God's creation it was natural for a woman to love a man in the spiritual sense, there was no need to carry that love to any physical realm. He used the example of Christ and Mary Magdalene."

Surprised by what Maggie had just told her, Theresa asked, "What did you tell him?"

"I told him that I was no saint and that he was not God! At that point, he told me to see this man I was speaking of, and to get my answer from him. Then he said that my sins were forgiven and told me to go in peace."

"Maggie, I can't believe you actually confronted him in a confessional. What was the question that he told you to ask this hypothetical man?"

"Well, I told him how much I loved him and I wanted an answer as to whether he loved me in return."

"You actually told him you loved him in the confessional, and you wanted him to tell you he loved you in the confessional as well, all the while he was performing the blessed sacrament of confession?"

"Yes, that pretty much sums up the situation and that's when he started telling me about love in the spiritual realm."

"But," Theresa stammered, "I guess there must be more to the story, as I've seen you both together and you both seem so happy. Has something more happened between the two of you? Did you ever get the answer to your question?"

"Did I ever," blurted out Maggie, "just before we left for New York, he told me he loves me and we agreed to delay any decision as to what we are going to do about it and our whole situation. We agreed to revisit it later to figure out what we should do next when we get back home."

"Wow, I guess I've been so preoccupied with what has been going on in my life that right under my nose, I didn't realize two of the people I love most in this world were falling in love."

"Theresa, you've had a lot on your plate to deal with that is so much more important than two confused and late-blooming idiots in love. You know, after regaling you with my story of a nun and a priest meeting and falling in love, let's get some fresh air and go to the hotel lobby and step outside and take in some of that New York atmosphere."

As they stepped out of the room, they were confronted by the papal guard and he immediately confronted them as to where they were going. He told them that Cardinal Roncalli asked that they remain in their room for the evening. Agreeing to abide by Cardinal Roncalli's wishes, they returned to their room at which point Theresa said to Maggie, "You've just added a new chapter to Gabriel's experiences in the confessional. Did I ever tell you about the time right after his first communion when he was about nine or ten? Years later my brother Daniel told me the story and my mother verified it was true."

"No Theresa, Gabriel never mentioned another incident or story he had in a confessional."

"Well, one Saturday morning our mother was washing clothes and as she did, she would check to be sure that the pockets of Gabriel's jeans were empty. When she came upon several pictures ripped out of a men's magazine of naked women, she immediately called Gabriel from his room and demanded to know what he was doing with these pictures. She admonished him for committing a sin for looking at those pictures. She asked him, how would he like it if other boys were looking at pictures like these of his mother and sister? She concluded by saying that Our Blessed Mother would be very ashamed of him and that he needed to go to confession to ask for God's forgiveness or he would not be able to receive communion on Sunday. She further demanded to know where he got these pictures and he told her that one of his friends found them in a tool box in his friend's father's garage. He told her that he and three other boys were all looking at them and his friend gave each of them some of the pictures. My mother was very upset with him and demanded she immediately drive him to the church, so he could go to confession. Before leaving, Gabriel searched his catechism to be sure he was confessing to the correct sin and was sure he had violated some form of the sixth commandment."

"Arriving at the church, our mother stood just outside the confessional intending to go to confession right after Gabriel. She heard Gabriel's nervous high-pitched voice saying, 'Bless me Father for I have sinned and I have committed adultery.' The priest, upon hearing this and knowing he was speaking to a child, was shocked. He asked in a calm manner, 'My son, with whom have you committed adultery?' My mother said that Gabriel's voice went another two octaves higher and he blurted out, 'With the other guys!' The priest, surprised by Gabriel's response, also blurted out loud enough so all near him could hear, 'With the other guys!' Gabriel became extremely nervous and frightened and said, 'Yes father, me and my friends were looking at pictures of naked women together.' The priest coughed loudly, and told Gabriel that he had committed a grave sin, but that he had not committed adultery and to have his parents explain to him about adultery. The priest gave him ten Hail Mary's and ten Our Father's and told him that his sins had been forgiven if he promised not to look at pictures of naked women and then told him to go in peace."

"Gabriel would kill me if he knew I told you about this happening to him as I think he was traumatized for a number of years after this happened. But, his brother Daniel loves to share this story to anybody who'll listen, and he tells it so much better than I do. The first time I heard it, he had me rolling in the aisles with belly laughs that to this day I've never experienced."

"Theresa, what a precious story; one of these days I'm going to find the right moment to tease him mercilessly about it. But, I think you and I better turn in for the night as you've got a big day ahead of you."

Chapter Ten

The governmental leaders of the world were concerned with the invitation being extended to the religious leaders. They feared the religious leaders would immerse themselves in the discussion of the angelic appearances and overwhelm the importance of the need to discuss the conflict of nations and the need to denuclearize the world. The U.N. Secretary General was up for the task and announced before the assembly that the safety of the people in the Middle East was their first priority. Secondly, the U.N. needed to provide safe relocation for those having to deal with the nuclear fallout, and to ensure that they would be medically and safely treated. His plan called for sufficient military troops to be deployed in these areas to maintain peace and security to thwart any effort by any one nation or several nations to take advantage of the situation for their own gain. He set an agenda to provide for separate meetings of the world leaders, apart from those of the religious leaders, so each could first meet to discuss their individual focus before having the joint session.

The presidential suite and adjacent conference rooms where the Pope was staying were suitable for his meeting with Cardinal Roncalli and his small group. They were seated in a small but ornate conference room waiting to meet the Pope. Gabriel and Sister Mary Magdalena took extra precautions to ensure that Sister Mary Theresa was comfortable. Cardinal Roncalli remained calm and affable as the Pope arrived. He greeted the Pope and his staff warmly as longtime friends and conducted the introductions with ease. It was the Holy Father who quickly took control of the meeting and asked all present to let him first speak with Sister Mary Theresa alone, as the others were ushered into an adjoining room.

When the door closed behind them, the Pope rose and stood before Sister Mary Theresa as he asked her to remain seated. He then fell to his knees and kissed her feet and said in Latin, "Bless you child for you walk with God." He then stood and placed his hand on Theresa's head and again in Latin gave her a blessing.

Theresa then knelt before the Pope and said, "Holy Father, I am not worthy to receive your blessing. I am a servant of our Lord and seek only to serve Him as I am humbled by your presence and pray for your good health each night."

"Thank you Sister Mary Theresa, it is I who am humbled. Come sit with me and tell me how our Lord has come into your life. Tell me about the events in Milwaukee, and what you know of the events in Somalia and Mexico in your own words."

Theresa knew immediately that the Pope had been briefed, but she did not know the extent of what he knew about her. But, she proceeded to tell him what she knew of the events that the Pope had mentioned. She took great care not to overlook any of the details and to ensure that the Pope understood her role in those events in Somalia and Mexico. She also ensured he understood that she played no role in the events that occurred in Iran.

The Pope sat quietly and listened and was attentive to her, ensuring that she was comfortable and at ease as he asked, "You have established a relationship with our Lord that is very special. He looks upon you with favor and though all of our prayers are heard by God, you are blessed to have the ear of our Lord when you pray. When you and Sister Mary Magdalena were confronted by the youths, did you say the words, 'Please protect us.' Then later, when you prayed to God regarding the priest and his congregation in Somalia, did you ask God to keep them safe? Then, the third time when the school children were held captive, did you ask God to keep them safe from harm? These are the questions that need to be answered as to whether or not you asked God to intercede in these events."

Theresa felt comfortable speaking with the Pope and was direct in her answer. "No Holy Father, I did not ask God to send His angels, but I did ask Him to protect us from harm at the hands of the youths."

"Do you recall using the words 'the Hand of God,' when speaking to the youths as a warning to them that God would protect you and Sister Mary Magdalena who was with you?"

"I believe I did, as the youths and Sister Mary Magdalena said that I used those words. But I did not use those words in my prayers regarding the priest and his congregation in Somalia or with the school children in Mexico."

"Do you understand that when you pray in these circumstances, you are in a way asking God to intercede on either your behalf or on the behalf of others, and that the angel's appearances are a direct result of your prayers of intercession?"

"Yes your Eminence, Monsignor Bonaci has helped me to understand that in those cases of the incidents in Milwaukee, Somalia and Mexico, I may have been the cause of the angel's appearances, but I knew nothing nor did I pray at all about the incident in Iran."

"So you do believe that the angelic visions were truly the appearance of one of God's angels, and other than the incident in Iran, do you believe that the angel came at your request?"

"Though I initially refused to believe that was the case, Monsignor Bonaci, Monsignor O'Grady, as well as Cardinal Roncalli assured me that no other explanation was possible. But, I know I had nothing to do with the appearance of the angel in Iran."

"Yes, I too believe that as well. But, the angel's appearance in Iran was actually not an intercession but an intervention by God Himself. An intervention is where God, seeing what is happening, intervenes in the natural order by injecting Himself into the incident on behalf of mankind without any request by humans. Do you understand what I am saying in acknowledging the difference between your prayers to intercede versus what happened in Iran? I'm sure that this was explained to you by Cardinal Roncalli. I understand from Cardinal Roncalli that our Lord has recently spoken to you and that you feel that I need to hear what the Lord has said. Would you now share with me what our Lord said to you?"

Theresa proceeded to relate the incident as it had occurred in her room at the convent during her evening prayers. She told the Pope that as she prayed to the Lord to help her understand what was happening to her, the Lord spoke to her. She described in detail the glow of lights, the brilliant sparkles, and then hearing the voice of the Lord. She related word for word what the Lord told her. Unbeknownst to Theresa, as she spoke of the Lord, a glow of light surrounded her, and the Pope while inwardly startled by what he was seeing, remained steadfast in listening to what Theresa was saying. It was at that moment the Pope knew beyond a shadow of a doubt that all of the information regarding Theresa was true. The documented reports as to the glow of light that surrounded her when she prayed combined with the levitation observed by others was confirmation to the Pope that she walked in the grace of God.

When Theresa had finished relating what the Lord had said to her, the glow of light surrounding her diminished. The Pope remained in awe as to what he had just heard and fell to his knees before her. "Thank you my child for sharing these words from our Lord with me. We must ensure that all on Earth are witness to hearing these same words. I want these words to come from you before the joint congregation of world governmental and religious leaders that will be broadcast live throughout the world."

Theresa was surprised by what the Pope had just said, and rose to stand before him as he continued to kneel. "My Holy Father, I am not the one that you should kneel before, kneel only before our Lord God. Please rise and help me to understand what I must do."

The Pope rose and went to the adjoining room and beckoned the others to rejoin him and Theresa. "Come join us, for we have much to discuss. Sister Mary Theresa has shared with me the words that our Lord has spoken to her, and we must find a way to share with the world our Lord's coming." As the others gathered around the Pope, he shared his other concerns. "The greatest obstacle will be the willingness of the religious leaders to accept the second coming of Christ. Because of the implication of the angelic vision over the Iranian nuclear explosion and considering that the target was Israel, the Jewish faith may now accept Christ's coming. They have believed that the Lord's coming was to be preceded by the wrath of God's vengeance on its enemies and may see this as the first coming. While there are those that may acknowledge that Christ is among the great prophets, they still may not accept Him as the Son of God and Savior of the world."

It was Monsignor O'Grady who spoke up, "Many will ask why the Lord is coming at this particular time. Think over the course of history, since Christ walked the Earth, of the great tragedies that have befallen man. Think of the evil that has been allowed to exist and grow stronger as millions of innocents have perished at the hands of evil by men and women. Why in all those years of great tragedy and great sorrow, while millions of those victims prayed, were their prayers not answered by God? God did not perform an intervention to stop the Nazis from killing millions of Jews. Nor, did God intervene in the corruption of His own church as millions were persecuted. Even today, millions of others suffer and die in concentration camps where genocide is practiced time and time again in every corner of the world."

The Pope listened to what Monsignor O'Grady was saying and replied, "Monsignor, you have spoken as a true religious scholar and I know that thousands, if not millions, share your concerns as do Monsignor Bonaci and Cardinal Roncalli. I too, as a young man, could not understand or fathom why God would allow man's cruelty to man to persist and grow. I too, believed that He would intervene and thought that if I served Him and devoted my life to Him, I would be better able to understand God's intentions. Monsignor Bonaci, you did not know you have a comrade in arms in questioning the will of God. What I do know is that God has allowed mankind to exercise his Free Will for man to determine his own fate in choosing what is good and what is bad. If mankind is to take their rightful place with Him in Heaven as God intends, then man must set aside evil, and end the hold that evil has on man."

"But," Gabriel interrupted, "why now has God intervened and not once or twice in the past two thousand years?"

The Pope responded, "Do you not believe that the founding of your very own country of the United States was an intervention by God to bring about the opportunity for mankind to find a way for man to help fight evil in this world. Did not your country end slavery, did it not end many wars and help thwart evil in its tracks. Think where mankind would be today and how evil would have persisted and grown if the United States had not intervened to stop this evil. Our God moves in mysterious ways and uses the Free Will of good men to right the wrongs that evil men continue to sow on mankind."

"But Holy Father," Monsignor O'Grady asked, "how will we be able to convince not only the religious leaders, but the governmental leaders as well, that God has spoken to Theresa and foretells of His coming."

"I believe," responded the Pope, "that the events of the recent angelic visions, together with the angelic vision over the Iranian nuclear site, will do much to convince everyone that God is now intervening into the affairs of man. The governmental leaders seem to have already acknowledged that the conflicts of men cannot be decided with nuclear weapons. Men must find a way to end their strife and their differences that have gone on for thousands of years. The very survival of mankind on this Earth is held in the balance, and God has shown that He is on the side of good and is prepared to wage war against evil. I also believe that when God spoke to Theresa of His coming, He did not specify a time when, in our sense of time, He would actually come. With God, His time frame is very different from the time frame of mere humans. The announcement of His coming may be a warning that the end time is near and that mankind must begin to prepare their souls for that time. Christ may be giving all of us a chance to use whatever time we have to accept that He is the one true way to our heavenly Father."

Cardinal Roncalli, who had remained silent listening attentively to the Pope, finally addressed the group. "Perhaps, God is warning us that we are entering the period of the Great Tribulation. This is the period before the Rapture that will be followed by Armageddon after which Christ establishes his millennial kingdom as Satan is defeated and condemned eternally and the Final Judgment comes. Our message must be that God is communicating with us, making known His active presence in the world through His angels, as foretold in the scriptures."

"For certain, God is telling us that He is done with allowing evil to grow and persist. He is also putting Satan on notice of what is coming, and it is now time for man to determine whose side they have chosen. Maybe we are entering some period of the Apocalypse in which God wreaks vengeance on evil and eliminates the existence of evil on Earth," concluded Monsignor Bonaci.

Later that day, the Pope sought to hold the religious leadership assembly in one of several Catholic cathedrals throughout the New York area. But, he could not achieve unanimity among all the religions that a church was a more appropriate place than a convention hall at the U.N. facility. Due to the many languages spoken among all of the many religions present, it was agreed to hold the meeting at the U.N. where each member through automatic interpretation could be accommodated. After vigorous debate, it was agreed that the Pope would be allowed to speak first in addressing the congregation to explain the angelic sightings that had recently occurred. It was further agreed that following the Pope's comments, each religious sect would have an appointed representative speak as to their interpretation of the angelic visions.

The next day at the assembly of the religious leaders, no sooner had the Pope asked for a moment of prayer to ask for God's guidance and blessing for all those present, than an outburst of commotion broke out in the hall. There was yelling and screaming by those assembled who called out loudly asking, 'Which God, or no God - whose prayers, or no prayers,' creating a complete pandemonium. Some started to leave, while others tried to restrain them, as shoving gave way to a near riot. The U.N. security forces in the assembly hall moved to halt the growing disruption. The Pope yelled into the microphone calling for each to pray silently or bow their heads in respectful silence. If this was to become a precursor of what was to come, the Pope became concerned as to the reception Sister Mary Theresa would receive when it was her turn to address those assembled.

One by one, each of the religious groups came forward. All the religious groups seemed to be posturing for their respective positions, seeking support from others. It was apparent that no compromise would be readily achieved as some of the religions' leadership had long ago succumbed to being controlled by their secular governments. They feared that anything that they said would not meet with their governments' approval. At the end of all their pleas by the various religious groups, it was generally acknowledged that the Pope and other Christian leaders would be expected to explain why the angelic visions had occurred. The Pope then requested that the members of the governments' leadership join with the various religious leaderships in the same U.N. hall to hear an announcement that would be important for all to hear as they gathered together. Within less than an hour, the full body had reassembled to hear the closing comments of the Pope. It was agreed that the joint assemblage would be televised worldwide live by all stations and on all media outlets.

The Pope remained at the podium and said, "I would like to say some words of encouragement for all in attendance. I have every belief that we will be able to achieve world peace and eliminate war and destruction if we recognize our humanity as a bond above all else. That bond is that the human race must be preserved and fostered. That religious freedom and religious tolerance must be universally accepted by all nations, states, regions, and areas. It must be agreed that the rights of one person, one nation, and even one religion shall not override or overshadow, and especially not control the rights of others other than what God has allowed. No one nation or multitude of nations can establish laws that enslave, restrict or forbid others from freedoms that God has bestowed on each man, woman and child. God has accorded all with the right of life, liberty, and equal treatment and equal protection not just under man's laws, but under the laws of God as well." Concluding with those words, the Pope asked that the assemblage permit Sister Mary Theresa to make her announcement before them. Despite cries of protests of denial, the congregation, primarily lead by governmental leaders, acquiesced to the Pope's request. Before Sister Mary Theresa could come to the podium, the Pope concluded "While you may not necessarily agree with what I have said, I sincerely hope that after you hear what Sister Mary Theresa shares with you, all will agree that we have arrived at a point in time where we can no longer disagree."

"It is my honor to introduce you to Sister Mary Theresa, who walks in the grace of God, and who will share with you how the angelic visions came to be. I ask that you give her every opportunity for her full message to be heard." As Sister Mary Theresa came to the podium the entire assemblage was silent. She spoke in a clear voice aided by the microphone so all were able to hear every word she was about to share. She began her story of the incidents in Milwaukee, and followed with what had happened both in Somalia and Mexico. She told of her prayers to God and how God had visited her and she then began to tell the assemblage what

God had said to her. As she spoke of God, a golden glow of light appeared around her silhouette and as she continued, she began to levitate to the astonishment of all present.

Suddenly and without warning, shouts from several areas of the assemblage began to be heard. "She is a witch, she is the devil's disciple, stone her" was heard as several attendees began to throw various items toward the podium. Several of the U.N. security forces rushed to protect Sister Mary Theresa, blocking several of the missile-like objects from striking her. Again, yelling, screaming and shoving caused some to start to move toward the exits as people fell and were being trampled. Suddenly all of the exits in the hall were locked by an unknown force as the huge main doors closed and locked by themselves. The entire hall was plunged into total darkness and everything became black. Just as suddenly, a glow of light appeared above the assemblage and the light grew in brilliance, overcoming the darkness surrounding those in attendance. As the light grew more brilliant, all began to shield their eyes and the hall became quiet and motionless as all stared at the orb as it grew larger and brighter. From the center of the orb appeared a concentration of sparkles of lights from which laser beams of light shot out in all directions.

Then, a thunderous voice from the orb was heard and the voice was understood in all languages by the assemblage. "I have come to restore peace throughout the world. I am the Alpha and the Omega. I am that I am. Who is, Who was, and Who will be forever. I am before all things and shall remain to be after all things for I am the eternal God, the Creator of all that exists. It is time to end all strife among you. I am the God of Abraham, Mohammed, and I am the God of Christ. I am the God that dwells in the spirits of Buddha and Hindu. I am the life that persists and abides in all living things. I call on my shepherds to reveal themselves to each of you to affirm that I am the one true God." Suddenly, sparks of light began to fly out from the orb forming figures of those shepherds. They could all see with their own eyes those shepherds from each of their religions who represented the prophets, their gods, and those spirits they held most high. The voice continued, "These are my disciples and shepherds, and throughout the time of man, each has been a source of guidance to bring you to know Me, and to know your way back to Me from the first day of creation. But, the Free Will of man has corrupted your beliefs with false prophets of man's making and has allowed evil to persist and grow to corrupt some of your beliefs. For too long, the depravity of man has allowed evil to hold sway and become the cornerstone of some of your beliefs. Evil has permitted you to believe that I, your only God, do not exist as evil has moved you away from the very purpose of your existence."

"In My love, you were created to join in spirit with Me that you might know Me and share in My abiding love for all that I have created. I placed man above all else in My creation. But, the depravity of man and his Free Will have sought in their finite nature to create their own gods. My divine qualities are beyond the comprehension of man and only when the spirit of man is united with Me in heaven, will man truly know the divinity of God. Often in the name of God, man's inhumanity to their fellow man has persisted for centuries. Due to man's Free Will, they continue to persecute each other, wage war, practice genocide, and commit horrible atrocities upon each other. These acts of persecution are not blessed by Me, nor does doing them in My name provide a gateway to heaven. Nor, will there be rewards for such behavior. These are the sins of man to feed their greed, their abhorrent behavior, and their corrupt and power-hungry ways."

"For thousands of years, false prophets and false gods attempted to portray Me with attributes that would strike fear in the hearts of man in order to control mankind and lead man into believing that those qual- ities were part of God's nature. I knew that the world needed a disciple who would set a standard of conduct where the qualities of forgiveness, kindness, love and generosity, together with hope, faith and charity would be recognized as the true nature of God. My commitment to man since your creation required more than just another prophet or disciple. My own divinity within the soul of man needed to be manifested in the form of a man to achieve the proper atonement for all the sins of man since the dawn of creation. But, that atonement by man alone in man's depraved state would not be a worthy atonement unless that soul was of both God and man. Therefore, from Me and within Me and in One with Me, and in One with the Holy Spirit was born Jesus Christ as the way for man to know his way back to Me. Christ, and He alone is the Savior and salvation of mankind. For thousands of years, man's depravity through their Free Will has persisted and has grown stronger as mankind has aligned himself with Satan. The faithful call Christ the Son of God; God made man. He and I are One and He is above all other prophets and disciples that have preceded Him and follow Him. He is the one true God of Abraham, Mohammed, Buddha, and of the Spirit of all Hindus and the many sects that seek God in their religion. Only the Son of God in His humanity could provide mankind not only a man that could be emulated as Christ, but that in Him, and through Him, man's spirit could attain entry into Heaven."

"Today, assembled here are the religious and governmental leaders of the world. To each of you much has been given and much is required. It is for you now to decide whether you are on the side of the one true God, or are you on the side of false gods, false prophets, and on the side of Satan. For you here present, the Day of Judgment has come for each of you to declare in your mind, in your heart, and especially in your soul by your own Free Will: Are you with Me or are you against Me?" Suddenly, the images of the prophets that God had presented to them grew in brightness and in unison declared, 'In my love of God here present, we declare that Jesus Christ is our Savior and the Son of God.' Suddenly, their images became flames as sparks whirled above the heads of those assembled and then came together into one brilliant orb as the voice of God was heard, "In heaven you have seen the unity of My prophets and their belief in Christ as the Son of God. Now it is time for you to decide. Do you stand with Me or do you stand with evil." Suddenly the voice was silent and the lights in the room returned to normal.

Immediately, many of the religious and governmental leaders began to speak at once as a few of them took to the podium to address the assemblage. "I do not know how all this trickery and deception was done. Whether by holograms, or by other technological means, some of you are attempting to impose your will on us and seek to enslave us in your beliefs. You are heretics and there are millions of us that do not follow Christ and His teachings. We condemn all Christians and will not respond to your treachery and attempts to put us all under the heel of the

Christian faith." One of the governmental leaders stated loudly, "Many of you by your Free Will do not believe in God and we support your right to choose whether to believe or not believe in a god or to worship or not worship as you please. Do not be tricked into some deception by offstage microphones, false sparkling lights of some hi-tech entertainment that attempts to make us dumbfounded and have us fall on our knees in humble obedience. As for me and the many of you that have not been taken in by this circus and have had your curiosity satisfied, we are leaving the conference. We feel sorry for those of you that have been blinded by your religious beliefs and have been taken in by this chicanery and deception by the Christian faith."

Many began to leave for the exits when suddenly the hall was again plunged into darkness. The flaming orb of light returned, even more brilliant than before, and it alone lit the room and the same loud voice returned. "Those of you that believe in me shall be saved and those that do not shall now perish." Immediately after the voice was heard, the room was again plunged back into darkness and a swirling wind could be felt as loud deafening clashes of thunder preceded the appearance of a huge angel from the brilliant orb dominating the entire room. The angel held out his flaming sword and from it laser beams of light danced all over the room for several seconds. Cries, wailing and the howling of hundreds of voices throughout the room were silenced. The flames from the angel's sword diminished and the vision of the angel was now only a glowing silhouette within the orb. Barely could be heard the prayers of the remaining faithful all kneeling in the huge U.N. assembly hall, as a wave of panic began to seep into their minds and hearts.

Suddenly, the lights in the hall returned to normal. It was immediately apparent that hundreds that were there before the angelic vision were now gone while hundreds kneeling in prayer remained. Among them, the Pope and Sister Mary Theresa were seen kneeling near the podium as Cardinal Roncalli, Monsignor Bonaci, Monsignor O'Grady and Sister Mary Magdalena knelt in prayer where they had been seated. The angelic vision then spoke, "You have seen the judgment and wrath of God, and now behold the Son of God." The angelic vision then disappeared and the golden orb returned and grew in brightness as the figure of a man hovering above them appeared. From His outstretched hands beams of light shown through the piercing of each palm and rays of light emanated from His pierced side. Christ then spoke in a gentle voice, "Each of you chose to believe in God and each of you will be given eternal life in heaven with My Father. Now all of mankind throughout the world knows what they must do with their lives if they are to be saved when the Day of Judgment comes. Henceforth, you will know that for the next one thousand years, peace will exist for you and your descendants. But, also know that for you and all of your decedents for the next forty generations, each will be judged more harshly on the Final Day of Judgment. If the covenant is broken that we have established here today, and evil is again allowed to enter your minds, hearts and souls, you and your generations will suffer the same fate as those that were condemned here today."

Suddenly, a golden glow of light surrounded Sister Mary Theresa, and Christ again addressed the assemblage, "Come Theresa, join Me in heaven for you have found favor with God our Father, and the Holy Spirit, and you have believed in Me as the Son of God and have accepted Me as your Savior." The faithful in the great hall and all those watching the live broadcast all over the world saw before their eyes, Sister Mary Theresa ascend from where she knelt to join the vision of Christ as He extended His hand to her and a burst of brilliant lights expanded throughout the hall as both then disappeared as the brilliant light immediately was extinguished as the lights in the hall returned to normal.

THE END

The Epilogue

More than three years have passed since the joint session of religious and governmental leaders and the Iranian holocaust. The world has become a different place. Nuclear disarmament was now well under way as the United Nations fulfilled the new tenants of its charter as a world peace organization. A new world order among all nations was created where the sovereignty of all nations was protected from one another. A new international code of conduct among all nations had been adopted. The United Nations was now the sole peacekeeping force settling disputes among nations through the World Court of Hague. The United Nations only intervened in internal disputes when a nation's efforts to resolve such strife was in conflict with the new United Nations Conference rules as to the treatment of a nation's citizens.

The strategic offensive weapons systems and large standing armies among all nations had been done away with. Only defensive weapons were allowed in order to protect citizens against crime and lawless bands of gangs. Trade among nations was established for fair and equal protection to ensure that no one or group of nations would upset the balance of needs, resources and assets of another nation. Advances in education, science, health, and technology were shared among nations with endeavors to reduce and eliminate disease, poverty, hunger, and homelessness.

Free and democratic elections occurred throughout the world as dictators and despots were removed from all leadership roles and jailed or executed for their crimes. Many others were tried and imprisoned who had permitted these leaders to allow and advocate torture, genocide, mutilation, or slavery. Some were charged with war crimes against humanity and were put to death. A treaty among all nations to protect the environment relative to land, air, sea, and space was adopted. The U.N. Human Rights Council not only ensured that the rights of all women would be equal to men, but also that human slave trafficking, illegal drugs, and female mutilation would be forever abolished.

Billions of copies of the DVD of the joint assemblage were made and given to each household all over the world, and were freely available for anyone needing one. The religious leaders of all religions reconciled ways to allow some freedom in establishing religious practices and customs. These freedoms would be consistent with the tenants that had been agreed upon by the world religious leaders at the joint conference.

A devout Christian U.S. President was elected as well as a devout Christian Orthodox Russian President. Communist leaders, radical socialists and radical Islamists across the globe were rejected by their people and replaced by newly elected democratic leaders. Christian conversions were occurring all over the world at unparalleled levels, especially among those in communist, socialist, and atheist nations. It seemed as though the world was now at peace and future generations of governmental and religious leaders were tasked with improving all areas of life to make them worthy of God's dictates in preparation of the Lord's return. The goal to eradicate evil was found to be a daily challenge as they awaited the Great Tribulation, Armageddon, Apocalypse, and End of Times that was to come when Christ returned to defeat Satan and condemn him for all time and cast him into hell for eternity.

The Pope, who had attended the joint session, decided to retire under the strain of the past few years in setting forth a new religious course of action to fulfill the new millennium. At the Conclave of Cardinals in Rome, Cardinal Roncalli was named the new Pope and chose the name Peter II to signify the last line of Popes. After calling for a new ecumenicalism among all religions, one of his first acts was to permit within the Catholic religion that priests would be allowed to marry. Also, the Church permitted that women would be allowed to be ordained as priests. Granting papal dispensation, he dismissed Monsignor Bonaci and Sister Mary Magdalena from their vows of celibacy, thereby allowing them to openly and officially acknowledge their love for each other. He officiated at their wedding at the Basilica in Rome joining them as husband and wife. Both now resided near the Holy Hill Convent and Cathedral in Wisconsin. Gabriel retained his position as Monsignor Bonaci and undertook the construction of a new chapel on the cathedral grounds dedicated to Sister Mary Theresa whose soul was being approved for sainthood.

Maggie, now no longer Sister Mary Magdalena, was now more than four months pregnant and asked Gabriel for a very special request. "Now that we know our baby is going to be a girl, I would very much like to name her Theresa, if you don't mind?"

Gabriel, showing his joy at the idea said, "Yes absolutely, that would be wonderful to have another Theresa Bonaci in the family. Then he continued jokingly, "We could even have a little Gabriel, a little Maggie, and a little Daniel."

"Yes, I'd like that very much," responded Maggie, as they both hugged and kissed, and each knew that Sister Mary Theresa was enjoying this moment as much as they were.

About the Author

Bruce J. Bonafide first gave serious thought of religion and a serious belief in God as he began his freshman year at Loyola University of Chicago. This Jesuit institution of higher learning required that in each semester a course in religion be undertaken resulting in each student literally majoring in religion in addition to their chosen course of study in some secular field.

In his sophomore year, he was given the opportunity to live near the school's North Shore Campus in what had once been a stately mansion along the affluent Lake Shore Drive area of North Chicago. Together with nineteen other students under the watchful and supportive eye of Father Donald J. Hayes SJ, a Jesuit priest, they founded Gonzaga Hall. This residence was dedicated to creating a brotherhood of Christian men who would hold mass each day and support a Christian way of life at the university. They held weekend retreats for singles and married couples looking to restore their faith in Christ as well as a desire to undertake a more in-depth philosophical study of the Christian religion.

It was at this time that the author gave serious consideration to the study of becoming a priest and the contemplation of the true meaning of life and his vocation. However, the author's interest in the study of political science, government, and law soon awakened other thoughts as to how he might live his life together with a strong desire to one day have a family of his own.

Seeing evil spread and grow, the author ventured into thoughts as to why God had not ended the existence of mankind on earth once salvation had been restored by Jesus Christ more than two thousand years ago.

These thoughts resulted in the author's senior thesis titled, 'The Martian Mary Theory.' In other words, salvation had come, and so why was man allowed to persist in succumbing to evil through his Free Will. How many more thousands of years would pass while evil grew stronger and evil was able to consume more souls. In support of his paper's conclusion, he was threatened with expulsion from the university just prior to graduation unless he modified the conclusion to conform to more Christian theological thought. Wanting to graduate with his class, the author soon devised a modified theory that allowed him to graduate. This experience soon gave rise to the author's interest in teaching classes in religious instruction to young men and women seeking to learn more about Christ in the years following graduation.

The author questions in his book, "The Intercession of God", why the prayers of the faithful for the elimination of evil in the world go unanswered. The fact that evil is allowed to persist was noted in the author's last novel, "The Money Mongers", a novel about the evil of greed for power, money, and influence in our society today.

Printed in the United States
By Bookmasters